More Ghosts
of
Georgetown

D0907654

ALSO BY ELIZABETH ROBERTSON HUNTSINGER

Ghosts of Georgetown

More Ghosts
of
Georgetown

Elizabeth Robertson Huntsinger

JOHN F. BLAIR
PUBLISHER
WINSTON-SALEM, NORTH CAROLINA

The paper in this book meets
the guidelines for permanence and durability
of the Committee on Production Guidelines
for Book Longevity of the
Council on Library Resources

DESIGN BY DEBRA LONG HAMPTON

PRINTED AND BOUND BY R. R. DONNELLEY & SONS

Library of Congress Cataloging-in-Publication Data
Huntsinger, Elizabeth Robertson, 1958–
    More ghosts of Georgetown / Elizabeth Robertson Huntsinger.
        p.   cm.
    ISBN 0-89587-209-9 (alk. paper)
    1. Ghosts—South Carolina—Georgetown County.   2. Haunted
houses—South Carolina—Georgetown County.   3. Georgetown County
(S.C.)—History.   I. Title.
GR110.S6H87   1998
398.2'09757'8905—dc21   97–46354

For Virginia Lee

Contents

Acknowledgments

I owe a great debt of gratitude to Captain Sandy Vermont, Phil Adams, Larry Williams, Leta Cribb Stearns, Chief Gene Martin of the Chicora Indian tribe, Ruthie Thompson, Eileen Weaver, William Baldwin, Bruce Mayer, Kathy Hemingway, Eleanor Moody, Mary Helen Yarborough, Glenda Collins, John Bellamy, Elma Moore, Catherine Lewis, Marguerite Assey, the staff of the *Georgetown Times*, the staff of the Georgetown Library, the staff of the South Carolina Historical Society, the Georgetown County Arts Commission, and my fellow members of the Huguenot Society of South Carolina.

For their skillful rendering of the *More Ghosts of Georgetown* manuscript into polished book form, I would like to thank Carolyn Sakowski, Steve Kirk, and Debra Hampton.

For his immense patience, love, and a wealth of knowledge about technical details, I am grateful to my husband, Lee Huntsinger.

Though my first book, *Ghosts of Georgetown*, was filled to the brim with ghostly legends, there are so many hauntings in Georgetown County, South Carolina, that I could not keep my chronicles from spilling over into another volume.

After that first book's publication, a number of Georgetonians came up to me and said, "Did you know there is a ghost at —— ?" They then proceeded to tell me firsthand—or to put me in touch with someone who could tell me—about another local ghost. It is the kindness of these Georgetonians, who cordially invited me into their homes or places of business and graciously spent time answering my questions and telling me about their experiences, that made a number of these stories possible.

After hearing about some of the twenty ghostly presences chronicled in *Ghosts of Georgetown*, many visitors to the town's historic district have asked me, "Why does Georgetown have so many ghosts?" The answer lies in the long and colorful history of Georgetown and the surrounding low country, in the vibrant nature of the people whose lives comprise this history, and in the area's vast expanses of water.

Water has been a hallmark in the diverse and fascinating story of Georgetown and its people. Indeed, Georgetown was founded in the early 1700s because it was an ideal site for a port. Water was also the reason six tribes of Indians thrived here, along the rivers and bay, for hundreds of years before the town came into existence.

Many of the ghostly legends of Georgetown are water-oriented, taking place on or near water. In some cases, the events leading up to a haunting were caused by perilous seas or fierce thunderstorms bringing torrential rain.

Georgetown is located on a peninsula where numerous rivers meet to form Winyah Bay, which opens into the Atlantic. The ocean also bathes the county's sea islands and mainland ocean-front property. The surrounding countryside is water-bound also. The Waccamaw, Black, Pee Dee, Sampit, and North and South Santee Rivers all flow eastward through the county toward the sea.

It is this proximity to water, coupled with the vital nature of many long-ago Georgetonians, that is responsible for the unusual number of hauntings and ghostly presences, I believe.

The ghosts chronicled in this volume all have legendary or historic reasons for haunting the places they do.

Some of these stories—such as those of the Pawleys Island terriers and the ghosts of Prospect Hill, Sunnyside, Woodlands, Keith House, Bellefield, Wedgefield, and Wachesaw—are well known and often told throughout the area.

Others are household legends that have scarcely been heard outside the immediate area where they took place. For example, nearly everyone in the small community of Lucas Bay has heard of the Lucas Bay light. Many of the older residents have even seen the phenomenon. Beyond Lucas Bay, however, mention of the light rarely brings recognition. Many Georgetown County residents know where the Hanging Tree is or have heard of it, but except for natives of Lamberttown and the nearby towns of Andrews and Jamestown, few know much about it. Residents of the fishing village of McClellanville have thrilled since childhood to the story of the ghost of the Cape Romain Lighthouse. But despite the occasional mentions of the tower's ghostly presence that appear in newspaper and magazine articles, most people are unaware of it. The many ghosts haunting Kinloch, while not exactly taken for granted, have long been considered a part of everyday plantation life by the people who live and work there. The Kinloch ghosts, however, have never before been written about. This, too, is the case with Bolem and Hemingway Houses, where family and friends have until now been the only people aware of the ghostly presences within their homes.

Many other Georgetown ghosts will never be chronicled, as they are presences that haunt without showing themselves. Others are viable ghosts with visible, audible manifestations, but no one can seem to find out who they were in life or what their reasons are for haunting. Still other ghostly presences are the deep, dark, well-guarded secrets of individuals who will not divulge their experiences. Sadly, their stories may never be told.

Elizabeth Robertson Huntsinger
September 16, 1997

More Ghosts
of
Georgetown

Woodlands

On the northern end of the Georgetown County coast lies the old fishing village of Murrells Inlet, a charming hamlet steeped in the history and romance of seagoing vessels.

From the creek, where the aroma of fresh seafood prepared by third- and fourth-generation chefs drifts out of time-honored restaurants, to the wharves, where commercial fishing boats unload the treasures of the deep, Murrells Inlet is a distinct blend of the culinary and the nautical. Many rambling restaurants line the inlet, blending easily into the rustic panorama of weathered wharves.

In the evenings, seafood lovers savoring fresh oysters, shrimp, scallops, and fish gaze over the tidal marshes to the Atlantic and the horizon. Venerable live oak trees, their storm-gnarled limbs reaching over the water, spread their huge, knobby roots across the creek-side land where buccaneers once walked.

There are many legends about the wary pirates who sought to avoid patrolling privateers by hiding in the labyrinth of Murrells Inlet's creeks. Edward Teach, better known as Blackbeard, is purported to have buried a cache of treasure somewhere in Murrells Inlet before meeting his fate off the North Carolina coast. Drunken Jack Island, located off Murrells Inlet, is named for a poor pirate accidentally left behind with a booty of rum stolen from a merchant ship. Surrounded by countless spent rum bottles, his bleached bones were found by his fellow crew members when they returned to the uninhabited island months later.

Named for Captain John Morall, who bought 610 acres here in 1731, Murrells Inlet has long been a haven for seagoing vessels and those who care for them.

The Civil War brought clandestine nautical activity to rival that of pirate days. When the Confederate commander in Charleston, General P. G. T. Beauregard, was in need of a seaport deep enough to get supplies into South Carolina when both Georgetown and Charleston were blockaded by the Federal navy, General James H. Trapier of Georgetown informed him that, at high tide, Murrells Inlet had nine feet of water over the bar. Blockade runners from Bermuda and Nassau were thus able to slip undetected into quiet Murrells Inlet and unload medical supplies and ammunition at Buck's Landing or Woodlands.

Built before the Revolutionary War, Woodlands was located on a low bluff above Woodlands Creek. It commanded a striking view of Murrells Inlet, the glistening stretch of beach across the inlet, and the ocean beyond.

Woodlands was a quintessential inlet home with clapboard siding and a wide, columned, wraparound veranda. Since most transportation was by water rather than by land in those days, the house was built facing the creek and the cooling breezes of the Atlantic. A narrow third story with a high window under the roofline gave Woodlands its lofty view.

A Murrells Inlet sea captain and his family lived at Woodlands during the years preceding the Civil War. This captain had no ship of his own and made a living piloting vessels for others. He was very experienced, having made voyages all over the world in extremes of weather. His judgment was considered excellent; he knew when to ride a storm out and when to take shelter. After sailing a vessel only a few days, he could tell how rough a sea or fierce a gale she could withstand.

On one occasion, the captain contracted with a wealthy low country plantation owner to sail a newly purchased schooner from England to Georgetown. The planter had bought the exquisite three-masted vessel from the estate of a British earl, who had spared no expense in building the schooner. Constructed in Aberdeen, Scotland, she was fitted out with every conceivable appointment.

After obtaining passage to Britain and locating the schooner, the captain realized he had never seen such a lovely vessel. From the finely carved captain's wheel to the well-appointed galley below, she was a study in shipbuilding detail. Copper and brass adorned the glowing, golden oak and the rich, deep-red Honduran mahogany of the interior. In the saloon, a small fireplace hosted a cheerily burning fire, before which a mahogany map table stood. The captain's stateroom was elegantly crafted with a mahogany dressing table built into the bulkhead and a trim mahogany bunk. In the galley, solid mahogany sideboards were built into the bulkheads flanking the companionway.

The most striking of all the vessel's exquisite appointments were her running and signal lights. Through handcrafted Venetian lenses, her lights glowed in brilliant shades of burgundy, emerald, and crystalline white.

After sailing the schooner to its new Georgetown berth, the captain understood that this was the vessel he had always dreamed of. As the rice planter paid him the handsome delivery fee they had agreed upon, the captain told him that if there was ever any reason to sell the vessel, he would like the first chance to buy her.

Several years later, the planter died, and the captain was able to buy the schooner from his estate. The day he brought his beloved vessel home to Murrells Inlet was one of the grandest he had ever known. His wife and children traveled to Georgetown with him to board the schooner for the ocean trip up the coast. Late in the afternoon, they made Murrells Inlet and at last secured the beautiful schooner at her anchorage in Woodlands Creek.

The captain was soon busy in the way he had always wanted, running charters with his own fine vessel after years of captaining ships for others. He took wealthy planters on long fishing trips to the Gulf Stream, returning after several adventurous days of hauling in king mackerel and swordfish and watching dolphins dance out of the ocean and chortle merrily to the fishermen. He took a load of fine Carolina lumber to New England, where it was awaited by master shipbuilders.

After a delightful spring and summer of owning, caring for, and captaining charters on the vessel, the captain refrained from taking charters of more than one night's duration. He watched the sea and sky constantly, for the gale season had arrived. During that time of year, devastating tropical storms could sweep out of the Atlantic with no warning whatsoever.

In late September, a fierce gale began to blow. With every hour, the wind grew stronger, causing the captain's immaculate schooner to dance at her mooring and repeatedly scrape her hull against the barnacle- and shell-covered pilings. At that point, the captain decided to anchor his vessel away from any pilings. But Woodlands Creek was too narrow to anchor her midcreek. And the captain was reluctant to anchor her anywhere that he could not have access to her as the gale grew worse.

As the howling winds increased, he made ready to take his beautiful schooner to sea in the face of what he recognized was a full-blown hurricane. Before casting off, he spoke urgently and

passionately with his wife. They both knew he was taking a tremendous risk by heading the schooner out to sea for the duration of the storm. Trusting her husband's skill and knowing there
was no other way to save the beloved ship, his wife tearfully
agreed to give the captain a bearing by keeping a lamp burning
in the third-story window of their creek-side home until his
return.

The captain kissed her good-bye and several minutes later
headed into the raging inlet with confidence, knowing that even
when he was out in the roiling waters of the Atlantic, he would
not lose sight of Murrells Inlet, that his beloved wife would
keep the lamp burning in the third-story window of Woodlands so he would have a fix even during the height of the
tempest.

The captain and his three crew members attempted to leave
the creek with the jib and one sail, but even this made managing the vessel in the vicious wind too dangerous. The tide was
falling as the crew hauled down the sail and jib and struggled
to secure them. Rather than take further risks attempting to
sail the schooner, the captain decided to let the outgoing tide
carry her through the inlet and out to sea.

As the schooner tossed toward the raging Atlantic, the captain's
wife strained to see her. Reaching for her brass telescope, she
focused on the vessel's vivid running lights. From that moment,
she kept the telescope trained on them as if her vigil would
keep the captain, his crew, and his ship safe.

Hours later, she lost sight of the running lights when the sea grew heavier during the darkest part of the night. She spotted the lights once again on the horizon, only to lose sight of them once more during torrential rains several hours before dawn.

As the first grey light of day edged over the now eerily calm Atlantic, search vessels were already headed toward the place on the horizon where the schooner's lights had last been seen. No trace of the vessel or her small crew was found floating in the ocean or cast up on the beaches, although search parties stayed out all that day and the next and the next.

The captain's wife remained hopeful. She knew a storm as fierce as the one just past could drive a ship to distant places. In years past, typhoon season on the Pacific had caused her husband to be more than a month overdue.

As months passed with no sighting of the schooner, it was gradually and sorrowfully assumed in Murrells Inlet that she and her crew were lost. No one voiced this to the captain's wife, though she may have thought the same herself. Still, she kept a light burning in the upper window of Woodlands at all times. Often, she sat by the light, wistfully scanning the horizon with her brass telescope, as had become her habit.

She did not see the lights of the schooner again until one year later, on the anniversary of the night of the hurricane. She quickly called her family members from downstairs. After seeing the lights, they called neighbors and friends closely familiar with the schooner. Though everyone agreed that the lights on the horizon were uncannily like those of the missing vessel, they were quick to add that they were undoubtedly those of a passing ship.

For the lights of a passing ship, however, these behaved curiously. They lingered long in the same spot on the horizon, not fading away until a few hours before dawn. It was at that time exactly one year ago, the captain's wife remembered vividly, when she had last seen the schooner's lights.

In the years thereafter, the captain's wife never failed to see the phantom lights on the anniversary of the storm, and she always kept a lamp burning in the upstairs window, as she had promised.

After her death, Woodlands lay vacant. As the decades passed, the yearly sighting of the schooner's lights on the anniversary of the hurricane and the lonely vigil of the captain's wife in the lamp-lit window became a fading legend.

Yet one September night many years later, a fishing boat carrying a party of men who were not from Murrells Inlet was lost in the ocean during a fierce storm. Having put out from the inlet that morning, they were unable to find their way back in the darkness until they fixed on a single bright pinpoint of light that helped them maneuver to safety. As the rain abated and the men came nearer to the source of the light, they saw that it emanated from the upper window of an old house on the creek.

Upon arriving safely but very overdue at the dock, they told the men in the rescue boats that had been out looking for them that, but for the light in the window of the old house, they would have been unable to find their way into Murrells Inlet until daylight. The rescuers, intimately familiar with the inlet, were quick to question which light and which old house the fishing party was referring to. When the fishermen pointed to the long-vacant Woodlands, sure enough, there was a light glowing in the upper-story window, a light none of the local men had ever seen before.

As Woodlands was supposed to be unoccupied, several men entered the house and made a complete search. Nowhere was there a sign that anyone had been in the dwelling in a very long time. In the story under the roofline, where the light had been seen in the window, there was no lamp and no indication of any sort of light source.

One of the older men looked out through the window and gasped in surprise. There, out in the blackness, were the brightly colored running lights of a vessel. He quickly drew the others' attention to the sight.

The older man realized that these must be the legendary ghost-ship lights he had heard about as a child. He then related to his companions the story of the lost schooner and the annual appearance of the lights. Perhaps the night at hand was the anniversary of the schooner's disappearance, he concluded.

Once outside and back on the dock, the men were again able to see the high window of old Woodlands. Once again, there was a light burning brightly.

After the fishermen were saved by the light from the upper

story of the abandoned house—from the window where the captain's wife had kept a lamp for so many years—Woodlands fell into disrepair and finally burned.

Still, the lights of the long-lost schooner continue to appear on the Atlantic off Murrells Inlet one night every September. They are the ghostly remnants of strong feelings that transcend time—the determination of a long-ago sea captain and the lasting faith he and his wife had in each other.

Woodlands stood off what is now U.S. 17 Business at the eastern end of Wachesaw Road on the bank of Woodlands Creek, now called Parsonage Creek.

Sunnyside

In the early evening, as the sun is sinking behind the massive, moss-draped live oaks that line the saltwater creeks of Murrells Inlet, lengthening shadows take over the low country seascape. Ordinary shapes assume spectral appearances as ghostly legends surrounding the inlet come to mind.

It was on a long-ago evening such as this that a murder took place, a cruel killing that has caused the restless victim to walk the inlet shores of Sunnyside, where she drew her last breath, ever since.

———

Sunnyside is normally as cheerful a house as its name suggests. Built in the early nineteenth century, when most travel was by water rather than land, it faces the waterfront. The facade, with its white columns and comfortable veranda, allows a panoramic view of Murrells Inlet. Though some say Sunnyside was constructed by Governor Joseph Alston for his legendary and doomed wife, Theodosia, it was in fact built by rice planter J. Motte Alston as a summer residence.

Alston bought land at Murrells Inlet from fellow rice planter Plowden Weston before the Civil War. Here, not far from Woodbourne, his rice plantation on the Waccamaw River, Alston made plans to build a creek-side home. He later chronicled the construction of Sunnyside and his years there in his memoirs. "It was a beautifully wooded tract of land, live and water oaks, magnolias and cedars, on a bold salt water creek," he wrote. "Here I built an eight room residence. The plan I drew myself."

His carpenter, a man named Richmond, managed the construction. "The frame was all finished at Woodbourne, moved across the river in flats and hauled to the shore by ox teams," Alston recorded. "Richmond did the whole work—of course with the assistance of some of my men to lift the heavy timbers. Of course, all the fine work, such as doors, windows, paneling, plastering, and painting was not domestic. I hired a New York builder to put up an oval stair way. Altogether the Sunnyside style of architecture was an improvement over that of Woodbourne.

"But Rome, as they say, was not built in a day," Alston continued, "so it consumed a winter and summer and a month or two over, to have our new home completed."

Sunnyside allowed the family to enjoy Murrells Inlet's creekside life while Alston remained a short distance from the duties of managing his plantation. "We were two miles from Woodbourne, and every day I would look after my planting interests and return to dinner," he wrote. "My table was most bountifully supplied; the plantation supplied all the poultry, etc.; and the deep creek in front of the house all the fish, oysters, clams, crabs, and shrimp, to say nothing of the game from both places.

"I was quite in love with our new home. And so we resided in our new home always 'til the first of July when we would seek a cooler atmosphere, either in the mountains or on Pawleys Island, some 12 miles below. In October we would return to Sunnyside."

As the years passed and his children grew older, Alston felt they needed more education than was available locally or through tutors. He decided to sell Woodbourne and its vast rice fields and move his family to Columbia. "As there was no inducement to live at Sunnyside which was only an adjunct to my rice plantation, I therefore sold the latter to my brother Charles," he recorded.

This sale took place less than three years before the Civil War.

Charles died impoverished shortly after the war, and Sunnyside was eventually sold out of the Alston family.

In the early 1900s, it was operated as a fishing lodge by Mr. and Mrs. William Avant. Near the end of August 1909, during the Avants' ownership, Dr. Grover Cleveland Bigham and his young wife, Ruth, residents of Harpers, South Carolina, vacationed for a time at Sunnyside. All was not well between the couple, for Ruth carried a terrible secret. She was almost certain that her husband's brother, Smiley Bigham, had murdered a young black man the previous month.

The murdered youth, Arthur Davis, had worked as a field hand for Smiley on the Bighams' farm in Florence County. One hot July afternoon, Smiley had accused Arthur of injuring a mule in the eye. After being struck down by the enraged Smiley, Arthur had run home to escape him. Smiley had then gone to the Davis home and told Arthur's mother that he wanted to punish her son. Fearful of Smiley, she told him she would no longer permit her son to work for the Bighams and that he had already left to seek other employment. She added that if her son had indeed hurt the mule, then the law, rather than Smiley Bigham, would punish him. Smiley coldly replied that Arthur had until sundown to come to the Bigham residence.

When night fell and there was no sign of Arthur, Smiley became upset. During a terrible display of temper witnessed by members of the Bigham family, including Cleveland and Ruth, who were visiting from Harpers, Smiley announced that Arthur would suffer as the mule had suffered.

He then left the Bigham household, sought out two other men, and went—masked and under cover of darkness—to the Davis home. Ignoring Arthur's mother's refusal to let them inside, the three men barged into the house and dragged the frightened young man into the night. They then mounted and rode away, hauling Arthur beside one of their horses.

After searching frantically all night, Arthur's mother found her son in the far reaches of the woods, his lifeless body battered by the dense underbrush.

The sheriff and the coroner examined Arthur's body at the scene. Noting the countless lacerations and bruises and beginning to assume the youth had died from loss of blood, they nearly missed the small drop that had coagulated near his ear. Upon closer examination, they discovered that a long nail had been driven into his head.

There was little doubt about who had perpetrated this heinous crime. During the abduction, Arthur's mother had recognized the voice of Smiley Bigham and listened as he and his companions had called one another by their first names.

The sheriff arrested Smiley and his two accomplices. But just as quickly, all three were released on bond. A trial for the murder of Arthur Davis was set for October.

Once Smiley was home, the Bigham family gathered in support of him. They all promised to swear he had not left home on the night of the murder.

They all promised, that is, except Ruth. Cleveland's young wife, who had finished college just two years earlier and taught school for a year before being swept off her feet by her husband, was unversed in the legendary murderousness and loyalty of the Bigham family. She naively announced that she would tell the truth if called upon to testify. The truth, she went on bravely, was that Smiley, after vowing to punish Arthur, had been away from home the night of the murder.

Out of Ruth's hearing, Cleveland assured the Bighams that there was no need to worry about Ruth's testifying against Smiley, because he would personally see to it that she did not.

Ruth soon traveled to Mountville in Laurens County, where she had grown up and where she had been teaching school when she met Cleveland. "Mrs. Bigham," the *Georgetown Times* later reported, "when at her old home some few weeks ago on a visit and receiving letters and telegrams from her husband to come home at once, expressed reluctance at the idea of going and even wept when she, pressed with the letters and telegrams, realized that she must return to her husband."

It wasn't long before Ruth was reluctantly home in Harpers with her husband, preparing for a trip to Sunnyside, the Murrells Inlet fishing lodge and boardinghouse run by Mr. and Mrs. William Avant.

Ruth and Cleveland were uncomfortable around each other at Sunnyside, to say the least. What would have been a peaceful, happy respite for most couples was for them a stay filled with angry words punctuated by long, stony silences. Ruth simply would not abandon her principles and allow her brother-in-law to get away with murder.

On Saturday, September 4, Ruth changed into swimming attire and threw her husband's long grey raincoat over her bathing costume. She knew that William Avant and Cleveland were on Sunnyside's front veranda, which overlooked the creek. So as not to draw the attention of her husband, whose ill mood she wanted to avoid, she did not walk out the veranda door but used a door on the side of the house. It was near dusk when she reached the water.

Meanwhile, Cleveland was laying a plan. In the two weeks that he and Ruth had been staying at Sunnyside, he had spent his evenings on the veranda with Avant, plying him with whiskey and stories of the ghosts that walked the inlet. Even now, they were ruminating about ghosts. Didn't Avant believe that Alice, the ghost of the young girl who haunted the nearby Hermitage, walked along this very creek? Such were the questions he asked.

Avant was superstitious but not normally afraid of ghosts. However, since Cleveland had brought the local spirits to his attention, Avant had witnessed them on two occasions. One sultry night, after being awakened by a slight but persistent rapping sound, he had seen a ghostly figure at his window. And just the previous night, while alone on the veranda, he had seen something pale and wispy rising from near the water's edge. Between these ghostly sightings and Cleveland's eerie tales, Avant was wishing that he and his wife, who was expecting their first child, could move away from the inlet.

On this balmy September night, as Ruth walked toward the

creek, Cleveland was busy convincing Avant that a ghost could be frightened away by firing shots at it. No one would be hurt, Sunnyside would be rid of its ghost, and Mrs. Avant and her unborn child would be safe, he said.

Through the wispy Spanish moss hanging from the live oaks between the veranda and the water, Cleveland and Avant made out a figure walking slowly to the creek. It was a phantom, Cleveland insisted, and they must shoot it to drive it away. Avant wondered aloud whether the figure was Ruth, but Cleveland replied that Ruth was resting in her room. The men went inside for a shotgun, returned to the porch, and advanced toward the water just as the figure bent down.

At Cleveland's insistence, Avant aimed his shotgun at the figure and emptied both barrels. As the men dashed back into Sunnyside, Avant had a horrible feeling. After a quick search of the house, he discovered to his horror what Cleveland already knew: Ruth was not resting in her room, nor was she anywhere in the house. The sickening realization that he had been duped into murdering an innocent woman settled over Avant like a shroud.

He and Cleveland grabbed a light and rushed back outside and down to the creek, where Ruth Bigham lay bleeding into the sand, barely breathing. Cleveland picked up his wife, then laid her back down. Two men who would later testify at the trial—one of whom was lodging at a neighboring house and the other of whom was camping nearby—rushed to the scene. Someone picked up the dying Ruth, carried her across the yard, and laid her on the veranda, where the blood pouring from the wound in her back soaked deep into the steps. She took her last breath on the porch of Sunnyside.

Avant went into Georgetown with the shocking news of Ruth's death and returned with a deputy sheriff and the coroner.

The detailed accounts of the killing of Ruth Bigham printed in the *Georgetown Times* and the *Charleston News and Courier* both ended with the verdict of the coroner's inquest: "The deceased came to her death by gunshot wounds, by mischance, at the hands of W. B. Avant, and G. C. Bigham as accessory thereto; both men laboring under great mental excitement and fear at the time of the deed." In both accounts, Cleveland and Avant were purported to have believed that Ruth Bigham was a burglar. They allegedly called out to her several times before Avant, at Cleveland's insistence, shot her in the back from a distance of twelve feet. Neither man was mentioned as having mistaken Ruth for a ghost. In fact, Cleveland said that before Avant fired, they had feared being shot themselves.

But word soon spread that Avant had fired under his and Cleveland's assumption she was a ghost.

A scathing article on the front page of the *Georgetown Times* on September 8 criticized the inquest jury for bringing a charge of manslaughter in a case that was so obviously a homicide. It also expressed surprise that "a young wife met a horrible death at the hands of two big men, in the light of day, because they were afraid of ghosts."

The front page of the *Georgetown Times* of September 25

carried an article citing the recent unhappiness in the Bighams' marriage. It also discussed the inability of friends of the deceased to believe Ruth's death was an accident.

The State carried statements from fishermen who had been near the scene of the shooting but had not been available for the inquest. These fishermen said that from their vantage point on the creek at the time of the shooting, they could easily make out Ruth Bigham to be a woman. If they saw her so clearly, the fishermen insisted, the men on the porch at Sunnyside, who were much closer to Ruth, surely saw that she was no ghost.

The trial of Cleveland Bigham and William Avant in the death of Ruth Bigham was scheduled for late October in Georgetown. Meanwhile, the trial of Smiley Bigham and his two henchmen for the murder of Arthur Davis was held in Florence County. The effort was futile. Several of the state's witnesses had left the area, and the families of the three defendants stated that the men had been in their homes on the night of the young man's death. Ruth Bigham never got the chance to testify about Smiley's determination to make Arthur Davis suffer and about his absence from home during the murder. Smiley and his cohorts were found not guilty.

The trial for the death of Ruth Bigham got under way on October 21 in the Georgetown County Courthouse. Designed in the Greek Revival style by Robert Mills and built in 1822 of sandstone-colored stucco over brick, the stately courthouse had been the scene of many memorable trials. Few, however, had garnered interest like the Ruth Bigham case. The prominent

Bigham family was legendary for its murderous deeds and the ease with which it escaped prosecution. Smiley had just gotten away with murder, and it appeared that Cleveland was about to do the same.

Among the prosecution witnesses were some who had not been present at the inquest, during which Ruth's death was ruled accidental. Prominent among them was a Mr. Smith of Mullins, who had been 120 yards away when he heard a shot. Upon hearing a voice shouting, "Bring light, have killed someone!" he had approached to see the trouble. At a distance of 30 to 40 yards, Smith testified, he had clearly seen the tragic scene on the beach. He also testified that the victim had been shot in the open at least 40 feet from any shrubbery, and that it had not been dark when the gun was fired.

J. D. Murchison of Marion, the man who had been camping near Sunnyside, testified that at the moment he heard the fatal gunshot, it had not been quite dark, and that he had been able to recognize a man in that light from sixty-five yards away.

Other witnesses corroborated the testimony of Smith and Murchison.

Despite having Congressman J. Willard Ragsdale as their defense attorney, Cleveland and Avant had little evidence in their defense. The jury pronounced them guilty of manslaughter. Refusing their attorney's immediate request for a new trial, the judge sentenced the two men to three and a half years' hard labor.

Following an appeal to the South Carolina Supreme Court,

Cleveland was released on a bail of fifteen hundred dollars. By the time it was discovered that he should not have been released due to the appeal's not being made during the required time, it was too late. Cleveland had fled, and his family members had cunningly deeded the holdings posted for his bail to other parties. Obviously, they had known Cleveland would flee. Avant was eventually released on bail also.

In April 1910, during the spring term of the South Carolina Supreme Court, the case was tried a second time. Again, Cleveland and Avant were found guilty. The time had at last come for them to go to the penitentiary, but they were nowhere to be found.

Avant had escaped to Texas, where he was soon recognized and apprehended. Returned to South Carolina, he served his sentence and was released in 1913. He returned to his wife and little girl, who had not even been born when her father was jailed for manslaughter. He did not, however, return to Sunnyside, but settled on a farm in Georgetown County. He continued to be haunted by the events of 1909. Avant went through periods when he failed to eat or disappeared for days. He died within a short time.

Cleveland Bigham remarried, fathered a little girl, and bought a house in Atlanta, where he had fled after his first trial. He kept in touch with his wily Bigham relatives in Florence County, secretly visiting them on occasion, staying in a secret, concealed room they constructed especially for his visits.

While the venerable Sunnyside continued to offer cheerful

respite to others, it held no comfort for the two murderers. Neither Avant, during the brief and tortured remainder of his life, nor Cleveland, during the long, clandestine years before his death, ever attempted to revisit the scene of the crime. They may not even have been aware that, shortly after Ruth Bigham's death, her ghost began to appear along the creek. Her eerie presence, first noted by fishermen and later by surprised neighbors, was whispered to have a purpose: she was seeking her murderers.

The lovely, innocent woman whose death was never truly avenged has not departed Sunnyside. Although her remains were buried many miles inland, the spirit of the pure-hearted Ruth, who died because she refused to lie and allow a young man's murderer to go free, continues to wander the creek where she was shot. Still clad in her swimsuit, with Cleveland's long grey raincoat modestly draped over her shoulders, her ghost appears at twilight.

For years, her mortal blood stained the steps leading down from the Sunnyside veranda where she died, a dark and tangible link to the fair spirit roaming the shore below.

Sunnyside is located on the Murrells Inlet waterfront, just off U.S. 17 Business.

Wachesaw

From Boston, Massachusetts, to the southern tip of Florida flows the East Coast's inland maritime passage, the Atlantic Intracoastal Waterway.

This two-thousand-mile route, built by the United States Army Corps of Engineers, is made up of natural inlets, sounds, bays, estuaries, and rivers linked by man-made canals. Venturing into the open Atlantic for a total of less than ninety miles, the Waterway is highlighted by twenty-two lighthouses and breathtaking, diverse passages.

Just above the Georgetown County line, the Waterway becomes one with the Waccamaw River. From there, river and Waterway flow to the port of Georgetown, where the Waccamaw ends at the harbor town's peninsula and the Waterway continues its path southward through Winyah Bay.

This Waccamaw River section has long been heralded by some as the most enchanting on the entire inland passage.

The dark, almost inky Waccamaw flows past miles of high riverbanks lined by ancient, moss-laden live oaks and long-fallen algae-covered logs where turtles sun themselves. Massive cypress trees grow in and tower over the swift-flowing river, the tannic acid of their bark and fallen leaves giving the fresh water its dark hue. Many of the cypresses bear huge, lofty nests in which ospreys—graceful, eaglelike raptors—raise their young.

The high riverbanks give way to lower sections where swamps stretch interminably under the sun-dappled green canopy. Here, great and small alligators, lazy in appearance but prepared for lightning-fast movement, lie motionless and watchful.

These swampy areas give way to miles of golden rice fields, where nineteenth-century floodgates lead into canals cut during antebellum days. Once carefully cultivated among the labyrinth of canals, the grain now grows wild, a delicacy enjoyed by migrating ducks, geese, and other wildfowl.

Wacca Wache Marina, a charming overnight stop for many yachts on their Waterway pilgrimages south in the fall and north in the spring, is part of the Waccamaw River's splendor. Many local craft and a colorful selection of "live-aboards" call Wacca Wache home. Other boats are launched into the Waccamaw at adjacent Wachesaw Landing.

Wachesaw Landing has long been the name of the village at

the end of Wachesaw Road. The village derived its name from Wachesaw Plantation, the vast rice barony that began the commercial use of the landing as a loading place for rice.

But where did Wachesaw Plantation get its name? Many say Wachesaw is the Waccamaw Indian name for "Place of Great Weeping," while others claim that its translation is "Happy Hunting Ground." No matter which is correct, both suggest a revered status. In fact, Wachesaw was an Indian burial ground long before the days of the rice plantations. On a high bluff overlooking the landing, undiscovered for two centuries by a succession of Wachesaw Plantation owners, lies hallowed—and haunted—ground.

———

The earliest Wachesaw owner of European descent is believed to have been John Allston, who received the tract as a Royal grant from the king of England around 1733. In 1748, Allston married his second wife, the widow Sarah Torquett Belin. After Allston's death, ownership of Wachesaw stayed in the Belin family until the early years of the twentieth century.

The Reverend James L. Belin was born in 1788. By 1825, he was the owner of Wachesaw. The plantation reached its pinnacle during his lifetime, producing six hundred thousand pounds of rice in 1850. Remembered best not as a plantation owner but as a distinguished Methodist clergyman, Belin preached to Indians and slaves. A circuit-riding minister overseeing five mission churches, he was en route to one of them at the time of his sudden death in 1859. This tragedy occurred as he was driving along Wachesaw Road, which ran the length of the plantation, then as now connecting Wachesaw on the Waccamaw River with Murrells Inlet on the Atlantic. Belin was killed when the horse pulling his buggy ran out of control, throwing him to his death.

Wachesaw was next owned by the Reverend Belin's nephew, Dr. Allard Belin Flagg. Dr. Flagg is infamous for being indirectly responsible for the death of his sister, the legendary young antebellum lady Alice Belin Flagg of Murrells Inlet's Hermitage.

After the Civil War, Dr. Flagg decided to tear down the Church of St. John the Evangelist, located on Wachesaw. As the church had fallen into disrepair, he wanted to dismantle it and use the lumber to build himself a summer cottage on the ocean at Flagg's Landing, now known as Garden City. Former slaves warned him of the impropriety of tearing down a church and using the lumber for a house. They then looked on skeptically as Dr. Flagg did just that. He had the cottage nearly completed when a fierce September storm blew it down. No sooner had he rebuilt the house than an October gale destroyed it.

The original Wachesaw plantation house, located in a grove of live oaks near the river, burned in 1890. The plantation was sold out of the Belin family in 1904.

In 1930, New York architect, designer, and industrialist William A. Kimbel, later an adviser to the Eisenhower administration, bought Wachesaw. In May of that year, while they were unearthing part of the riverbank in preparation for building a hunting lodge, workers made an amazing discovery. There, on the bluff overlooking Wachesaw Landing, was a hallowed Waccamaw Indian burial ground that had lain undisturbed for centuries.

The burial ground was excavated to reveal countless vividly hued Spanish beads and thirteen skeletons arranged in a circle. All the remains were of women and children except for two adult male skeletons of remarkable stature. The feet and legs of the skeletons pointed to the outside like the spokes of a great wheel, the skulls forming the innermost part of the circle.

In February 1937, during preliminary work on the site of Kimbel's permanent Wachesaw residence, another circular grave site was unearthed on the riverbank. A number of enormous burial urns were found. Inside each urn was a skeleton, painstakingly interred in a crouching position. According to Indian lore, this allowed the deceased to leap into the hereafter.

Excavations continued under the direction of the Charleston Museum. Other burial urns were soon found. They had been carefully buried in circles like the other urns, but in layers of three, with the top two layers in tighter circles, so that they formed a kind of pyramid toward the surface of the ground. Also discovered was a skull full of the type of beads brought by early Europeans to trade with the Indians. These relics indicated that the burial ground was probably used during the time of early Spanish exploration.

Some burial mounds held only the skeletons of children. What could have caused the demise of so many Indian children at once? During the excavations, case after case of diphtheria was diagnosed in the local community, until the number of those stricken reached epidemic proportions. Many believed that the germs had lain for centuries at Wachesaw, only to be unearthed during excavation of the Indian graves. Although others refused to believe this, it is a fact that many germs can survive for hundreds of years. It is also a fact that untold numbers of Indians, particularly children, died after coming into contact with European diseases such as diphtheria, for which they had no resistance.

Relics were carefully removed to the Charleston Museum. A flint sharpener, stones for grinding corn, spoons, and bracelets were among the many small items unearthed.

Some workers, however, were unable to resist the temptation to steal ancient artifacts.

One man decided to keep some small Indian relics to treasure privately at home. Four arrowheads and three spearheads found their way into his deep pockets.

In bed that night, he was awakened by deep, mournful cries and wails, but he managed to go back to sleep. The same cries woke him the following night, but sleep was a long time in coming again, for he saw two unusually tall and muscular Indian braves looking through the stolen arrowheads and spearheads. For four more nights, the worker's sleep was interrupted by wailing and the appearance of one brave or another. On the sixth night, he was so frightened by the appearance of several braves at once that he remained awake until dawn. At first light, he gathered up the arrowheads and spearheads and took them to the excavation site to wait for the archaeologists from the museum. He presented them with the relics and was not awakened from his sleep again.

Another worker pocketed several beads, planning to sell them for a tidy profit. He also stole other revered relics from the graves: the beautifully preserved teeth of Indian children. Pleased with his stealth and greedily planning how to spend the profits of his thievery—for he had heard the museum workers discussing the value of Indian antiquities—the worker hid the beads and teeth in a closet in his home. However, he was kept from sleep that night by wailing and the voices of children speaking in a tongue he had never before heard. After a few sleepless, fearful nights, he, too, returned the relics and was visited by the voices no more.

Despite the care the archaeologists took in removing the Indian skeletons, burial urns, and relics to the Charleston Museum, nothing could erase the fact that the sacred burial site had been defiled. Many Murrells Inlet residents will attest that moans and wails still emanate from the site of the old Waccamaw Indian burial ground on the bluff high above the river.

> *Wachesaw Landing is approximately 20 miles from Georgetown; it is located down Wachesaw Road from Murrells Inlet. The plantation house built by William A. Kimbel on the Indian burial ground was disassembled in 1985 and replaced by a residential complex.*

Pawleys Island
Terriers

Many summer visitors return to Pawleys Island year after year to enjoy the blissful ambiance of this diminutive sea island linked to the mainland by two narrow causeways. Some have been making an annual pilgrimage since they were children, as their parents, grandparents, great-grandparents and great-great-grandparents did before them.

For a century, two tiny dogs have returned summer after summer to frolic with happy abandon on the seashore of this four-mile-long, half-mile-wide island, where they spent their happiest hours. Devoted to each other in life, these little terriers who died long ago still cavort at the edge of the Atlantic. Often mistaken for lost dogs by those seeing them for the first time, they are well familiar to longtime residents, who know why the terriers appear for such a short time, then disappear without a trace.

——————

Once the seasonal haven of antebellum rice planters, Pawleys Island saw an increase in summer visitors each decade after the Civil War. During the late 1800s, many Georgetonians spent a portion of the long, hot summer on Pawleys savoring the cool sea breeze coming off the Atlantic.

As the turn of the century neared, steamships stayed busy plying the Waccamaw River between Georgetown and the island, bringing boatloads of cheerful beachgoers from town as well as from other parts of the state. Most travelers from outside Georgetown journeyed into town by train and were taken from the station to the steamship dock by horse-drawn buggy. From there, they boarded the *Janie*, the *Ruth*, the *Madge*, the *Pelican*, or other local steamers. Often, the steamships were filled to capacity with island-bound passengers. Hearts soared and spirits lifted, for the travelers would soon be at Pawleys!

Though a number of families owned homes on the island and moved there for the summer, many visitors rented houses during the season. Still more stayed at seashore hotels and boardinghouses. Though the Ocean View Hotel and the Pawleys Island Hotel hosted many turn-of-the-century guests, perhaps the most popular destination was the Winyah Inn and the accompanying Winyah Inn Cottages, known simply as "Mrs. Butler's," after the hospitable owner and operator.

Once ensconced on the island, the summer people spent their

days bathing in the ocean, fishing, shrimping, and crabbing. Their nights were filled with social and sporting activities. The evening itinerary at Mrs. Butler's during the first week of August 1898 included an oyster roast on Monday, a library party ending in a dance with live guitar and violin music on Tuesday, a literary and social night on Thursday, and a crabbing party on Friday. Dances were held at Mrs. Butler's and various island residences on Saturday night. In one such home, the lanterns had to be hung on hooks, since the force of so many people dancing caused lanterns placed on the mantels to be vibrated onto the floor.

Other evenings were spent gigging flounder in the creek between the island and the mainland. Night gigging involved patiently plying a slow-moving rowboat as the light of a wood torch burning in a flat metal pan attached to the side of the boat illuminated the dark creek bottom. Sharp-pointed gig poles were poised expectantly above the water, waiting for the second that an elusive, flat-bodied flounder was spotted.

Lunches and suppers were usually highlighted by the fresh seafood that abounded. A typical menu at Mrs. Butler's consisted of an immense smorgasbord including turtle soup, oysters on the half shell, clam soup, and summer duck. Breakfast often featured a highly coveted delicacy: sea-turtle eggs. Morning beachcombers delighted in discovering the distinctive tracks of a mother loggerhead turtle and would follow the trail to the nest of precious eggs laid during the night. Before the eggs had a chance to mature and hatch, the nest would be robbed bare of its dozens of distinctively shaped eggs.

Many children were among the seasonal islanders. They stayed in summer homes or boardinghouses with their parents. A July 1897 edition of the *Georgetown Semi-Weekly Times* mentioned that there were twenty-five children staying at Mrs. Butler's.

In the family atmosphere that prevailed on the island, many youngsters were allowed to play in the sand and at the surf's edge with little supervision save that of older children. This care-free summer practice resulted in a near-tragedy that brought heartfelt praise and grateful attention to two heroic little turn-of-the-century terrier dogs.

One balmy Saturday afternoon, as the salty breeze cooled the blazing sand of the wide Pawleys Island beach, a group of children was busy just below the high-tide line digging and piling sand to construct an elaborate castle. Conditions were perfect. The tide was about halfway out, assuring that the castle would not be washed away before evening. Enough water was left in the sand from the high tide that, by digging the castle's moat deep enough, water would appear at the bottom of the trough. The sand was damp and easy to form into walls, bridges, and turrets.

The older children, more expert and serious about sand-castle construction than the younger ones, commanded the project. Smaller children were allowed to participate as serfs, following orders of where to dig, where to put more sand, and when to haul water for the moat.

The youngest was a cheerful toddler boy more interested in

knocking over the older children's carefully constructed walls than in helping make them. It was the well-understood duty of the little boy's older siblings and companions that they were responsible for his safety when playing on the seashore. To keep him busy and to prevent him from destroying their growing sand castle, the older children gave the toddler a little bucket and shovel and persuaded him to dig in the sand on his own near where they were working.

Happy at first to have his own project, the little boy soon lost interest in digging and decided to wade into the surf and get some water in his bucket, as he had seen the older children do. Treading determinedly across the sloping beach toward the foamy tidal flow, he was unnoticed by the older children.

Never having walked in the pull and tug of the surf without his hand firmly held by someone larger, the little boy became unsteady on his feet as the outgoing water sucked the sand from under them. The receding tide and the heavier-than-usual surf soon combined to pull the toddler's feet out from under him. Within seconds, he was rolling helplessly. Despite the shallow depth of the water he was in, each outward roll of the surf pulled him several feet farther, until it seemed he would be lost in the ocean. An older person would have simply fought to sit up and then risen out of the rough surf, but the bewildered toddler was rolled like a piece of driftwood.

More than likely, no one would have ever been sure of his fate had not two terriers intervened. Mildly curious at the little boy's trek to the ocean's edge but razor-sharp alert as he lost his footing and fell, the dogs began barking furiously as he was rolled to and fro in the shallow surf. They rushed to the group of children working on the sand castle and barked with all their might. The children, familiar with the terriers, paid little attention until the wildly barking dogs ran into their midst, wrecking part of the castle. The youngsters leaped up, aghast at the destruction of their labor and surprised, too, for these terriers were not usually disruptive.

One of the older boys, his focus now averted from the sand castle, spied the toddler rolling helplessly in the surf. Crying out, he rushed to the water, followed by his playmates and the frantic terriers. The oldest children soon had him safely clasped. Realizing that the little boy could have been pulled out to sea without their knowledge was very sobering to the children, who had not known a care in the world just moments earlier. Overwhelmed with relief, they cuddled the toddler and praised and petted the terriers, which had ceased barking the second the child was out of the water. They now wriggled with delight, reveling in the attention they were receiving for their lifesaving deed.

A dance was held at one of the boardinghouses on the island that night. By the end of the evening, nearly everyone on Pawleys Island knew of the terriers' heroism.

No one was prouder than the lady who owned them. The male terrier and his smaller female mate were her greatest joy. She brought them along every summer to her family's house on the island. The family had several dogs, but the terriers were her favorites and her constant companions. She kept them impeccably bathed and groomed, fed them from the table, and talked to them as if they were human. She had spent many hours training them and positively reinforcing their good behavior, with the result that they were exceedingly obedient and well mannered. She included them in as many of her family's activities as was practical and safe. Disciplined and nurtured as intelligent, sensitive creatures, the terriers—as nearly all dogs will when treated so—developed intelligent, sensitive personalities.

Morning and evening, no matter what the weather, the lady walked her terriers along the shore. Although they had the freedom to leave the veranda of the family's oceanfront home, cross the high dunes, and romp on the beach at will, this did not equal the pleasure they took in their twice-daily walks with their mistress.

The terriers would race into and out of the shallow water, sometimes paddling seaward for a few minutes before making their way back to shore. There was no end to their delight as they romped with one another, snapping at the foam that always evaporated in their mouths and chasing the shorebirds that never failed to fly out of reach just in the nick of time. They never seemed to run out of energy as they pranced and played during these walks, showing off wildly for their beloved owner.

The day after the terriers saved the toddler, a hurricane swept the coast. It did not make landfall near Pawleys Island, but the gale-force winds, the raging rain, and the danger of hurricane-spawned tornadoes and waterspouts kept everyone on the island securely indoors for two days. The third day dawned with clear blue skies and a stiff breeze that seemed placid compared to the hurricane. At last, it was safe to frolic on the beach once more!

The mistress was delighted to finally have a stroll on the shore with her dogs. The terriers, friskier than ever after having been confined, gallivanted at the edge of the ocean, paddling out and back repeatedly, each time swimming a little farther.

While swimming toward shore, the male terrier was suddenly engulfed by a tremendous wave that came up behind him. Tired from his forays into the ocean, he was unprepared for this onslaught and was rolled under the wave. The fierce undertow then sucked his struggling little form back out, allowing him no chance to come to the surface for air.

Meanwhile, the other terrier did not bark but ran, tail tucked between her legs, up and down the hard-packed sand near the spot where she had last seen her mate. The mistress, fearing her pet was tiring, had been calling him in when the wave overtook him. When he did not surface after being engulfed, she became frantic. She, too, ran up and down the shore adjacent to where she had last seen the dog. Her eyes strained for a glimpse of his dark head, but he had disappeared.

After more than an hour, the lady returned sadly to her house, carrying the remaining terrier in her arms, for it refused to leave the shore on its own.

Late that afternoon, the lady crossed the sand dunes to walk along the ocean, as she did nearly every day. Only now, there was a lone terrier instead of a pair, and both mistress and dog were very sad indeed. Instead of frolicking on the shore, the terrier walked slowly and listlessly at her mistress's side, occasionally raising her head to gaze dolefully at the ocean.

All at once, the little creature was filled with energy. She raced across the shore to a dark mound partially covered in wet sand. The terrier dug rapidly and quickly unearthed the cold, wet form of her companion. When the lady caught up to the dog, the terrier was pulling her lifeless mate along the sand toward her mistress. Tears fell unchecked from the lady's eyes as she knelt to caress the wet, sandy fur. Slowly and sadly, she walked back to her house cradling the lifeless dog in her arms. She felt even worse for the remaining terrier, which barked happily and danced around her feet, thinking her mate was being brought home.

A pall fell over the entire family, which sent for a carpenter to build a tiny wooden box. The family lined it with soft blanket material before closing the little form away.

Rather than burying the terrier on the island, the family members took the coffin back to their plantation on the mainland, where they interred the little box in a quiet area of the garden. As the summer was nearly over, they decided not to return to Pawleys Island for the remainder of the season. This decision was not entirely for practical reasons. None of the family wanted to spend time so soon at the place where the cherished pet had died.

The surviving terrier suffered a worse bereavement than

anyone in the family. Day and night, she whined and pawed the door until she was allowed outside, at which time she went straight to her companion's grave. The grieving dog could not be persuaded to leave the site, but had to be carried away no matter how long she had been sitting there. Nor could the dog be persuaded to eat. Despite all the love and tender care lavished upon her, she fell deeper into melancholy.

After less than two weeks, the lone terrier died, lying forlornly on the grave of her beloved mate. Another wooden box was made. Soon, there were twin graves in the garden. Petite marble stones were made to commemorate the final resting place of the two heroic dogs.

The following summer, the family made its annual move to Pawleys Island. Although everyone still missed the terriers, their quiet sadness had evolved into a wistful nostalgia. The terriers' mistress was now able to remember them with a smile rather than with tears.

Not long after the family's arrival, the nanny from a neighboring oceanfront house called on the mistress. She told the lady that her dogs were playing unattended on the beach. The nanny had been about to leave the shore with her young charges when the terriers had run down to the water near the delighted children. She had called the dogs but had not been able to get them to come back to the houses. Reaching the top of the dunes with the children, she had turned to call the dogs once more, but they were gone. Knowing that the lady would not want her dogs running loose, the nanny had come to tell her of their whereabouts.

The lady could not help smiling fondly at the description of the dogs. Appreciating the nanny's concern, she told her that these must be the pets of another, for hers had died nearly a year ago.

As the summer progressed, however, reports of her free-running terriers came to her from children who had played with the dogs during previous summers. These were the same dogs, the children innocently insisted, except that they played without barking and disappeared before they could be petted.

Still assuming the terriers in question belonged to another summer family, the lady began hoping to get a look at them. One evening, she was sitting atop the highest dune separating her home from the seashore, having just returned from the west veranda of her house, where she had watched a spectacular sunset over the creek with her family. She had just settled down on her high, sandy perch to view the twilight over the Atlantic when two dancing, prancing little creatures caught her eye where the surf met the hard-packed shore. Her terriers! Without another thought, she ran down the dune calling the dogs' names.

At the sound of her voice, the terriers stopped abruptly and pricked their ears. Then, in one motion, they bounded toward their mistress and ran in huge circles around her, pausing only to leap into the air and prance on their hind feet.

Arms held wide, the lady laughed out loud as the lively pair frolicked silently around her. When she was sure they must be exhausted and ready to lie down panting, they vanished! As far as she could see up and down the empty beach, no dogs were in view.

Many more times during the summers of her long life, the lady saw the terriers. Each visit was unexpected. She saw them by moonlight, in the heat of the afternoon, and in the misty early morning, but most often at twilight. Never was she able to touch them or hear their barks, but the dogs never failed to cause her heart to sing with joy. Fleeting as their appearances were, the dogs always appeared vibrant, alive, and exuberant.

Over the years, the lady and her family passed away. The house they summered in became the seasonal home of others who loved the island. The terriers, however, continued to frolic silently on the stretch of beach where they had once romped with their mistress and become heroes for saving the life of a helpless toddler.

Now, a century later, island residents who have heard the legend of the terriers know the fruitlessness of trying to catch these frisky creatures and return them to their owner. The phantom dogs and their mistress are occupants of another time in the genial history of Pawleys Island.

Pawleys Island is located 15 miles north of Georgetown on U.S. 17.

Prospect Hill

Loved and cherished through the last two centuries, Prospect Hill is home to the ghosts of a pair of former owners from two very different times in the plantation's history. One ghost is that of a benevolent mistress from Prospect Hill's glory days. The other is from the forlorn post–Civil War years, when the plantation was close to being lost by a man who desperately wanted to keep it.

Low country rice production increased following the Revolutionary War. More and more planters settled along the rivers of

Georgetown County to cultivate the lucrative golden grain. They built elegant plantation homes overlooking the dark waters. Lush gardens and hundreds of acres of rice fields kept the plantations thriving. The planters entertained lavishly and traveled extensively. Most of them owned several fine homes in diverse locations in addition to their plantation manors. It was not uncommon for a planter to own a home on one of the sea islands off Georgetown, an "upcountry" or mountain retreat, and townhouses in both Georgetown and Charleston.

During the grand days of the eighteenth century, Prospect Hill rose magnificently from the fertile soil along the Waccamaw River. Owned as a separate property first by Joseph Allston, born in 1735, the plantation was left to his son Thomas, born in 1764. Shortly after the Revolutionary War, Thomas married his cousin Mary Allston. The couple built the two-story Prospect Hill manor house and, with the help of an English gardener, landscaped elaborate formal gardens adjacent to it.

Thomas died in 1794, leaving Mary a childless widow with a 550-acre rice plantation. Once she began managing the property, Mary soon knew most of Prospect Hill's more than five hundred slaves by name. Though slaves on some other plantations were treated badly, Mary soon became legendary for her benevolence.

After several years, she married Benjamin Huger, Jr., the son of Major Benjamin Huger, a Revolutionary War hero. A politically important man of French Huguenot descent, the elder Huger had hosted the Marquis de Lafayette in his North Island home during the war. Benjamin Jr. was a prominent political figure as well, serving in the Sixth, Seventh, Eighth, and Fourteenth Congresses of the United States. He was also a member of the South Carolina House of Representatives in 1798 and 1799 and from 1808 through 1812. A member of the South Carolina Senate from 1818 through 1823, he served as that body's president from 1819 through 1822.

After a summer tour of New England to celebrate their marriage, he and Mary settled into a busy but blissful union at Prospect Hill. They traveled widely in political circles and hosted important persons at the plantation during the early 1800s.

Their most notable social and political honor came in 1819, when Prospect Hill was an overnight stop on the national tour of President James Monroe. The fifth president of the young nation left Washington on March 30 to visit the country's most influential cities. His entourage included Secretary of War John C. Calhoun of South Carolina and his wife and children; Samuel Gouverneur, the president's private secretary and future son-in-law; and Major General Thomas Pinckney, who would host the president at his El Dorado Plantation on the South Santee River.

The party was met at the South Carolina line by a governor's aide and a committee from All Saints Waccamaw. Traveling by carriage, it reached Prospect Hill on the morning of April 21. After a full and joyous evening of dining and entertainment, the party spent the night. The members awakened the next morning to a splendid breakfast, then prepared to embark for Georgetown, where they would enjoy another day of grand events in the president's honor, including a welcoming address written by Benjamin Huger.

Departing Prospect Hill, the presidential party walked on a fine red carpet the Hugers had laid from the steps of the manor house down the entire terraced quarter-mile bluff to the canal, where a plantation barge waited. The barge soon cut through the dark waters of the Waccamaw with flags flying proudly, lavishly decorated in red, white, and blue. It was poled by livery-clad servants.

Benjamin Huger, Jr., did not live a long life. When he died in 1823, Mary found herself a childless widow in charge of her great plantation once more. Doubting now that she would ever raise a family, she threw herself into the continued development of Prospect Hill's gardens and the welfare of her beloved servants.

Some years later, Mary was diagnosed with a rare, incurable, lingering disease. She did not cloister herself away, but worked even harder to make sure Prospect Hill and all who lived there would prosper after her death. When her illness finally forced her to remain near her bed, she took to spending as much time as possible on the small upstairs portico near her room. From this vantage point, she could look down upon her life's work and be seen by the slaves she was too weak to join outside.

In addition to grieving over their mistress's illness, the servants at Prospect Hill dreaded what might become of them after she passed away. Since Mary had no children to inherit Prospect Hill, the cruel facts of slavery dictated that they would have a new master when she was dead and buried. The new owner might treat them just as kindly as "Miss Mary" always had. Or he might treat them indifferently or cruelly. Or he might divide Prospect Hill, selling the slaves to distant plantations and tearing apart their families. They might even have a master who lived elsewhere, leaving their fate in the hands of a hardhearted overseer.

Mary's death in 1838 cast a pall over Prospect Hill, a sad silence punctuated only by the mournful spirituals sung with great feeling by her hundreds of slaves. During the nights following her death, small groups of them gathered at the boatman's house, located between the manor house and the Waccamaw River at the head of a canal. Sitting beneath the stars on the wood-plank landing, they sang and prayed, pondering their fate. The comforting sight of the light that had long burned in Miss Mary's bedroom was gone, leaving the dark facade of the mansion as a poignant reminder of her passing. Those who were old enough to remember back nearly two decades reminisced about the grand visit of President Monroe.

On one of these nights, a slave gazed toward the darkened mansion and, to his surprise and awestruck delight, saw the glowing figure of a lady who could be no other than the beloved Miss Mary standing on the upstairs portico.

Dressed in flowing white and illuminated by the moonlight, the figure was not frightening, for she was a familiar sight to all the slaves. Many nights during the years preceding her death, they had seen Miss Mary standing alone on her portico in her white nightclothes, gazing across the Prospect Hill gardens toward the river. To see their beloved mistress once more was a sign, the slaves knew, that she was still caring for them and that their home was secure.

Shortly thereafter, all of Prospect Hill—slaves included—was purchased by Colonel Joshua John Ward of Brookgreen Plantation. Being familiar with the integrity of the Ward dynasty, the servants knew they had no worries as to the new owner's treatment of them. They were immensely relieved that their homes and families would remain intact.

Of course, the slaves who saw the loving ghost of Miss Mary and celebrated the Wards' ownership of their home had no way of knowing that they and their children would be free men and women within three decades. Neither did they know that a Ward heir would come to love Prospect Hill so much that he would rather die than lose it.

After the Civil War, without slave labor to work the fields, many rice plantations slid into despair. Despite the efforts of owners to work the vast fields once tended by hundreds of hands, no low country plantation was able to approach the amount of rice yielded before the war. Although there were a number of moderately successful postwar planters, the halcyon days were over.

Many planters gave up and moved away, selling their plantations and seashore residences at low postwar prices. Others sold everything except their declining plantations and stayed on. They struggled to make a living with the help of former slaves who did not want to leave their lifelong homes and now worked for their former masters for wages. Unable to maintain the rice fields that had made them wealthy, some destitute planter families raised chickens and grew vegetables on their formerly manicured front lawns just so they could have food. Many families lost their plantations for lack of money with which to pay property taxes.

Although Colonel Joshua John Ward had died in 1852, his vast holdings were not dispersed to his eleven children until 1867, after the Civil War had ended and every child had come of age. At the time of his death, the tremendously wealthy Ward had been one of the largest slaveholders in the South, but the war had vastly depleted his empire. In order to fulfill his bequests to his daughters, the family's spacious Charleston townhouse and their beloved summer retreats—a mountain manor in Flat Rock, North Carolina, and a cottage on Pawleys Island—had to be sold. A plantation was given to each Ward son, according to the colonel's will. The son who was heir to Prospect Hill fulfilled his father's wish that a Ward should one day inherit what the childless Hugers had left behind.

Owning Prospect Hill after the Civil War was vastly different from the lifestyle in which the young Ward heir had been raised. His primary responsibility was simply keeping the plantation out of bankruptcy. There were no lavish entertainments or luxuries. Faithful servants still lived at Prospect Hill, but their work was bought, not owned. The heir made a written agreement with the former slaves that he would support them until the crops were harvested. In return, the freedmen would work the plantation and receive half the crops.

The young heir faced the possibility of losing Prospect Hill forever. Taxes on the estate were long past due, and he still had to support the workers and pay all other expenses. The income he needed to meet his debts would not be received until after he brought in his rice crop, and the harvest was still months away.

In hopes of raising money to save Prospect Hill, he and Charles, his faithful manservant, journeyed to Charleston to seek a loan. Money was extremely difficult to come by during those dark days of Reconstruction, but the heir was determined to find a source. As he and Charles crossed river after river on the numerous ferry trips required to reach Charleston, his hopes rose. Surely, one brokerage company or bank would extend credit for a property as fine as Prospect Hill.

Alas, nowhere in Charleston could he find help. After being turned down by every financial institution in the city, he called on the villainous high-interest moneylenders, carpetbaggers who had set up shop temporarily in the low country to prey on people in financial need. But even the carpetbaggers would not help the heir of Prospect Hill. Already heavily mortgaged, the plantation was too deeply in debt to bear the burden of yet another loan. Even could the heir have secured one, the interest being charged by even the most lenient of banks was too high in comparison to the modest income the plantation would generate in the near future.

Despondent, he made one last stop in Charleston before beginning the journey home. He entered one of the city's many saloons to soothe his dejected soul with the balm of rum. Besides a bottle, the young heir found a lively card game. Northern soldiers still quartered in the war-ravaged port city were merrily gambling the late afternoon away. Hoping for some diversion from his problems, the heir joined them, sitting in on one hand, then another and another. Caught up in the chance for a windfall, he gambled boldly and, with one last unfortunate hand, lost what precious money he had. He left the saloon with a rum bottle on credit, the worried Charles riding by his side.

Long after midnight, they arrived dejected and tired at Prospect Hill. The heir did not feel the peace he always experienced when entering his beloved home. The place was now tinged with sadness, for he felt he had exhausted all chance of keeping it. Slowly, he bid Charles good night and turned, bottle in hand, toward the stairs. Concerned with his friend and employer's dejected state, Charles insisted that the heir wait until he had prepared something for them to eat, as it had been many hours since they had consumed anything except rum. The young heir quietly turned down the offer, telling Charles to eat alone. Before going to his quarters, he added ominously, "There is no point in me eating tonight."

Worried over the heir's state of mind and refusal to eat, Charles was scarcely able to consume more than a few bites himself. Rather than going to his cabin, he decided to check on his dejected friend.

He quietly climbed the stairs and stepped softly along the hallway until he reached the heir's door. Squatting to peep through the keyhole, he saw that a lamp burned beside the rocking chair where his friend sat. The dejected heir was slowly rocking back and forth, occasionally raising the rum bottle to his lips for a slow pull of the fiery liquid.

Ever more concerned, for the heir was not one to sit up all night, Charles decided not to leave his friend alone. Tired enough after the day's long journey to sleep almost anywhere, he curled up on the heart-of-pine floor outside the door and was soon asleep.

Waking within the hour, Charles peered through the keyhole once more, expecting to see the heir fast asleep in the chair. Instead, he was still slowly rocking, a fathomless expression on his face, his eyes staring into space.

Charles lay down and slept once more, only to be awakened an hour or so later by the sharp report of what sounded like a gun. Leaping up from the hard floor, he rushed to the door and turned the knob without bothering to peer through the keyhole. Hoping that what he feared was not true, he tore into the room. What he saw would burn in his mind for the rest of his life. In the grey light just before dawn, the lamp flickered beside the heir's still-rocking old chair. The poor heir lay on the floor, his pistol clasped in one hand and his blood spreading around him.

Cradling his friend's head in his lap, Charles gazed sorrowfully at the blood flowing from the mortal wound. "Why did you do this?" he murmured over and over as he tried in vain to stanch the flow of blood.

Raising his dimming eyes to Charles's tear-filled ones, the heir managed to murmur, "I will never leave here."

With that, he closed his eyes and lost consciousness. Blood soon ceased to pour from the wound, for the heir of Prospect Hill was dead.

Charles raised his head and heard the predawn calling of songbirds. Suddenly, there was silence. A cool, light wind from the river blew softly in the open window as the low flame of the lamp, still burning within its glass globe, flickered and went out. An owl hooted somewhere in the darkness. The rocking chair, which had finally ceased its motion, began slowly to rock once more, leading Charles to dwell on the heir's last words.

Years later, a number of declining low country rice plantations were bought by well-to-do Northerners who came to Georgetown County to hunt. Finding the old rice fields a haven for ducks and the forests teeming with deer, quail, wild pigs, and other game, they saved many fine antebellum plantations from dissolution.

Such was the case with Prospect Hill. The plantation's Northern owner and his wife, deciding to remain in the low country a large portion of the year, set about beautifying the manor house and gardens, which were soon restored to their former glory.

The servants at Prospect Hill, long familiar with the fate of the young Ward heir, were reticent about cleaning the room where he had died. However, it was now to become the bedroom of the new mistress of the house, so they were no longer able to avoid it.

Rumors began trickling into Georgetown about the chair that rocked by itself in the room where the tragedy had taken place. Some servants sensed a distinct presence there.

The mistress moved her bedroom to another part of the house.

A little pet dog was said to become very upset in the room, barking and pacing with hackles raised, its agitation directed toward a specific spot, as though an unseen person stood there.

A servant, alerted by one of the little dog's tirades, stepped into the room to see if she could discover what was upsetting it. Standing before her was a gentleman planter with pistol in hand. The long-deceased heir looked as if he had never left this life.

Quite taken aback but too shocked to have fear, she asked him what he was doing.

His reply, before he disappeared before her eyes, was simple: "I will never leave here."

Prospect Hill lies several miles northwest of Georgetown on the Waccamaw River.

Bellefield

When Belle Baruch bought the plantation of her dreams, she did not consider it unusual that the property had borne her name for two hundred years. Neither did she find it unusual—or daunting—that the manor that once stood on the site had a haunted history.

Ever since childhood, Belle had led a remarkable life. Born in 1899, she was the first child of famed Wall Street millionaire financier and presidential adviser Bernard Baruch. The Baruchs kept a luxurious Park Avenue apartment in New York, summered in Europe, and spent Thanksgiving through Easter at their coastal South Carolina plantation retreat, Hobcaw Barony.

Hobcaw was granted by the king of England to Baron Carteret during colonial days. After the Revolutionary War, the estate was sold and divided into thirteen rice plantations, one of which was Bellefield. Beginning in 1905, Bernard Baruch bought up ten of these holdings—Bellefield among them—thus making Hobcaw Barony a single entity once more.

Belle considered Hobcaw her home. Growing up the privileged child of a wealthy New Yorker paled for her beside her role as the outdoorsy daughter of Hobcaw's "baron," as Eleanor Roosevelt later called Belle's father.

Belle and her younger brother and sister, Bernard Jr. and Renee, roamed Hobcaw at will. The family's rambling Victorian mansion, Friendfield House, stood on a bluff across the water from Georgetown, overlooking the point where the Waccamaw River widens into the broad expanse of Winyah Bay.

Under the tall hardwoods and evergreens not far from Friendfield House, the children had their own miniature house for play. From the outside, it appeared to be a modest adult dwelling. But upon closer observation, it was apparent that it was a well-appointed house for small people. The windows, the doorways, the furniture, and even the kitchen were child-size.

Belle cooked her first meal in the miniature kitchen—a whole roast turkey for her parents. Bernard and Annie Baruch never got to sample their little girl's culinary masterpiece, however. Belle's dogs ate the meal while their young mistress was hurrying to the big house to invite her mother and father to dinner.

Bernard did not allow the intrusion of a telephone at Hobcaw. Twice a day, he had mail and telegrams delivered to his retreat via Georgetown. His close ties to the financial and political centers of the nation meant that Wall Street and Washington had to be able to contact him.

Belle was acquainted with the famous and powerful people of her day. Claire Booth Luce, Winston Churchill, Churchill's daughter Diana, and Franklin D. Roosevelt all spent lengthy vacations at Hobcaw as guests of her father. Many of Bernard's Wall Street and Washington associates came to Hobcaw to relax and to hunt deer, wild pigs, turkeys, quail, and ducks.

An avid hunter herself, the adventurous Belle once shot an alligator, although she preferred to stalk more traditional game. When she killed her first deer on the plantation, at the age of twelve, it was reported in the *New York Herald*. Belle often took advantage of moonlit nights to lead guests hunting on horseback.

Friendfield House caught fire during Christmas dinner in 1929 and burned to the ground. Bernard replaced it in 1931 with a more austere brick mansion, Hobcaw House.

Belle bought Bellefield Plantation from her father in 1936. The plantation had no house, but on a low bluff was the foundation of an early-nineteenth-century home that had burned before it was ever lived in. It was upon this long-ago base that

Belle built her own elegant manor house.

With its numerous chimneys rising among the surrounding live oaks, rambling Bellefield House was made to look like an old plantation home. Clapboard siding and contrasting dark wooden shutters added to the antebellum air of the home, concealing such modern appointments as a bomb shelter.

An accomplished equestrienne, Belle spent many hours in her plantation's practice ring preparing her horses for events in France and Italy. During most of the year, she kept these prize thoroughbreds in Bellefield's picturesque stable, a rambling white clapboard structure with a belfry. When the season arrived in Europe, Belle took her horses across the Atlantic by ship to participate in international steeplechases. She did not limit herself to highbrow activities, participating in charitable events such as donkey racing at a children's fund-raiser in France.

Foremost among Belle's horses was Souriant III, her Anglo-Arab, Normandy-bred favorite. This fine animal drew attention and admiration wherever Belle took him to compete. In pre–World War II Germany, the Nazis asked Belle to sell them Souriant so they could present him to Hitler as his personal horse. Belle declined. In Spain, officials offered to buy Souriant as a gift for their country's leader. Before turning the Spaniards down, Belle jokingly asked them how much money was in the Bank of Spain.

Enamored with air travel, Belle became a pilot, acquiring licenses to fly single-engine planes and copilot twin-engine aircraft. Her small red plane soon was a familiar sight above

Georgetown. No one in town was ever alarmed to see her plane disappear into the trees at Hobcaw across Winyah Bay. They knew the daring mistress of Bellefield was descending homeward to taxi down her own runway toward her custom hangar. She flew her father to various engagements around the Southeast. It was even rumored that Belle helped the Army Air Force with local surveillance during World War II, when German submarines patrolled the Atlantic dangerously close to Georgetown's shores.

Belle lived happily there for many years until her death in 1964. Having purchased the entirety of Hobcaw Barony from her father in 1956, she willed the property, including Bellefield, to the state of South Carolina for research and teaching programs. This gift guaranteed that Hobcaw's 17,500 acres of marsh, forest, and pristine beach will remain a refuge for the wildlife that thrives there.

Her house still commands the bluff, looking cool, lovely, and unapproachable at the head of the green expanse of Bellefield's manicured lawns. Her beloved Souriant is buried on the front lawn. His stall has been empty for many years, as has the practice ring. Hobcaw Barony's deer and feral pigs, the descendants of animals that were once the prized objects of hunts, meander on the estate's eighty miles of unpaved interior roads.

Bellefield was made famous by Belle Baruch and her legendary father, but what of the antebellum home on whose foundation Bellefield House was constructed? Who started the house on the bluff, and why was it never lived in?

Herein lies the story of Bellefield Plantation's ghost.

————————

During the halcyon decades preceding the Civil War, dozens of legendary plantations were established on Georgetown County's Waccamaw Neck. From Murrells Inlet south to Winyah Bay, plantation gentry lived lavishly beside the flowing black water of the tree-lined Waccamaw. Vast fields of rice, the life-blood of Georgetown's economy, flourished alongside the river. Each field was traversed by miles of canals painstakingly dug and maintained by field hands. The rice grown in these fields was like gold. It brought great wealth to a number of Waccamaw Neck planters.

The lovely, privileged daughter of one of these dynasties, groomed from birth to wed into her generation of plantation heirs, was given in marriage to Thomas Young, a youthful and ambitious planter who had no established manor house or rice fields. However, he possessed prime, fertile land on the southern tip of Waccamaw Neck and a burning ambition to create a plantation there.

Entrusted with the hand of his elegant, sheltered princess bride, he was determined to make a home comparable to the one she had been raised in. Before dawn each day, Young was out supervising and laboring in his rice fields. He worked tirelessly all day. After dark, he did not rest but went straight to the site of the manor house he was building for his wife. His nightly lamp-lit inspection of the day's work on the house was rarely cursory. He usually ended up with a hammer or a plane in his hand. A true perfectionist, Young savored knowing every facet of his plantation home as it rose from its foundation.

Late each evening—often in the early hours of the morning—he would fall into bed for a few hours of rest before rising ahead of the sun again.

While at first merely tiring, this schedule began to take a toll on Young's health. He lost weight and developed deep, dark circles under his eyes. Normally vigorous in appearance, he began to look pale and strained. Still, he did not lessen his schedule; the plantation and the house came before all else.

When the interior was nearly finished, Young intensified his already grueling schedule, working even later into the night. In the dark hours, the flickering light from his lantern could be seen on one floor of the house, then another, as he inspected the day's work and added his own.

Late one afternoon, Young was unable to swing himself into his saddle after a day in the rice fields. He collapsed on the ground beside his animal and had to be carried to bed.

That night, he sank feverishly into a coma, from which he never awoke. In three days, he was dead.

His wife of such a short time could not bear to move into the home her late husband had so lovingly built for her. The very sight of the graceful structure filled her with guilt that she had not realized her beloved was working himself to death.

All activity on Bellefield Plantation ceased. The slaves were sold to nearby plantations, and the rice fields lay fallow. The manor house was abandoned. Flickering late-night lantern light no longer shone from the carefully constructed window casements.

After a few years, though, boat passengers on the Waccamaw River began noticing light coming through the trees from the vicinity of the abandoned house. Midnight poachers, hunting illegally on the private land surrounding the house, noticed a light in the house, too, and began avoiding the area. Seeing a flickering light move from room to room was too eerie for even the most hardened illicit hunters.

Late one afternoon, a slave named Caleb who had escaped from a nearby plantation sought refuge in the manor house. A former Bellefield slave, Caleb was quite familiar with the grounds. In the years since the plantation had been abandoned, he had heard enough about the mysterious light that shone from the desolate windows to be certain no one would come looking for him there. Not only would searchers be leery of exploring the abandoned structure, they would also figure that a runaway slave would avoid the place. That made the house a perfect place to hide. He would much rather face a mysterious light than risk being caught and taken back to the plantation he had left.

Caleb lay down to rest on the floor beside a window in an upper-story room. The wide, smooth pine planks beneath him were warmed by the late-afternoon sun that shone through the windows. He fell asleep almost immediately.

When he awoke, the floor was cold and the room was in darkness, save for a faint light emanating from the stairwell. Sleepily, he raised himself on one arm. As the light gradually grew brighter, he sat bolt upright. The flickering glow was moving up the stairs.

At first, Caleb was overcome with a paralyzing disappointment. He had been found, and his pursuers were making their way to him. As the light grew brighter and reached the top of the stairs, he braced himself for the sight of his captors. Then he came to a sickening realization: no footsteps accompanied the light. No one was that stealthy. The light was approaching in utter silence.

Caleb slowly stood and readied himself for flight or defense. He held his breath, then recoiled in shock as a lantern emanating a bright glow—with a familiar form holding it—came around the corner of the landing. Illuminated in the flickering glow was the long-dead master of the house! He looked straight at Caleb and continued past him silently.

Caleb was horrified. There was no mistaking that face—he had seen it in life many, many times. All those eerie rumors of the manor house's ghostly lights were true, he realized, yet he had not believed them. He had come alone to this deserted place and met a haint face to face.

He walked swiftly down the stairs and out of the house, taking care to shut the door behind him. Steeling himself to walk—for haints were known to chase those who fled—Caleb made sure he was out of sight of the abandoned house before he broke into a run. He then made his way back to his home plantation and turned himself in.

No one else ventured into the abandoned house for several

years, although boat passengers on the Waccamaw continued to report seeing mysterious lights.

Many years later, the house burned to the foundation. No lights were ever reported after that, even by Belle Baruch and her guests at Bellefield House, constructed on the same site.

The Hobcaw Barony Visitor Center is approximately 2 miles north of Georgetown on U.S. 17.

Hemingway House

Eighteen miles inland from Georgetown lies the town of Andrews, established during the late Victorian era.

Like many Southern coastal towns, Andrews came to life around its railroad. The Georgetown and Western Railroad emerged in the western section of the county due to the area's rich pine forests. The lucrative trade in lumber and turpentine persuaded a number of people to settle what is now the western part of Andrews around 1880. The busy village was at that time called Harpers, after Edwin Harper, the owner of many local businesses.

The eastern end of what is now Andrews was laid out around 1900 by Captain Walter Henry Andrews, who called his settlement Rosemary. In addition to selling lots for businesses and homes, Andrews and the Rosemary Land Association donated land for churches and schools.

In 1909, Harpers and Rosemary decided to join and applied for incorporation. The new town formed by their merger was named Andrews in honor of Captain Andrews. An early mayor of the town, Captain Andrews was instrumental in bringing the Seaboard Railroad—which ran from Hamlet, North Carolina, to Savannah, Georgia—through Andrews. The town grew as train traffic increased. Many railroad workers and their families moved in.

Some of the oldest homes in town are beautifully maintained examples of the Victorian architecture in vogue all over America at the time Andrews was begun. One of these turn-of-the-century gems has more of a Victorian essence than even authentic period architecture can bring, for one of its former owners—a true Victorian lady—has never left.

Hemingway House, built about a hundred years ago, is fronted by a charming garden, above which rises a wide veranda with Ionic columns. This graceful home was built by the Heinemans, a Georgetown family that came to Andrews with the railroad.

The Heinemans did not live in the house long before it was bought by Basil Hemingway and her husband, William. Raising her two sons and two daughters and tending her exquisite flower garden, Basil might have lived to a contented old age had not a tragedy taken place: one of her young sons was killed in an automobile accident.

After this sad event, Basil's time on earth was not long. She died peacefully in her bedroom in her beloved home, the victim, it was said, of a broken heart. She had gone to be with her son. Sadly missed by friends and family, Basil was memorialized with a beautiful window bearing her name upstairs in the sanctuary of a nearby church.

The present-day Hemingways living in Basil's lovely old home are her descendants. They have long known the story of Basil, her love for her family, and her carefully tended flower garden, but they never guessed that her kindly spirit might be near until just a few years ago, when their young son was approaching the age of the child Basil mourned so long ago.

Basil's presence first became apparent when Elaine, the lady who helps clean the house, asked Kathy Hemingway, "Do you ever feel like someone is watching you?" When Kathy asked Elaine to elaborate, she explained that while cleaning the bathtub, she had turned around and seen a shadow, although no one was there. In fact, no one was anywhere nearby.

Kathy knew exactly what Elaine was talking about, because the same thing had been happening to her. "I had felt the same thing," she said. "It was very noticeable. I would be in the laundry room and see someone go by and step out to tell them something, and no one was in the house. After that, it became very evident. Right after that, I heard someone call my name, then call my name again. I came out and looked, only to find that I was here by myself."

Upon hearing of her mother's experience, young Katy Hemingway said she had heard her name called, too. Like her mother, she had found that no one else was in the house.

Kathy's husband's office is located on one side of the laundry room. Like countless doors on old wooden houses, the door to this office cannot be opened or shut without making a very distinct sound. The sound it makes when opening is markedly different from the closing sound. Soon after the first mysterious events, Kathy heard the sound of the office door opening, although no one could possibly have been in the office.

All this activity was centered in the hallway that opens out from the bathroom, the laundry room, and the office. It was in the same vicinity that Kathy and Katy looked up from watching television one night and saw a distinct shadow, although no one was anywhere near.

What is the significance of this area? The hall opens into the spacious, sunlit room that was once Basil's bedroom—the room where she died. Now the cheerful den of the Hemingway family, the room where Basil's spirit departed her earthly body has been graced by her presence once more.

Kathy believes her youngest child and only son, Ned, is the reason Basil has returned. "Ned is the only Hemingway grandson," she explained. "Basil's son died, so she is going to take care of mine. She is a very kind and gentle woman. Usually, spirits come back to right a wrong. Hers came back to protect."

Soon after Basil was established as an ethereal fixture in the household, Kathy was speaking with someone at church who was dubious about the spirit's presence. In light of the spirit's benevolent nature, it was suggested that Basil was an angel, to which the doubtful party replied that angels were already in heaven.

"All of a sudden, we had a very bad storm," Kathy said. "We went upstairs in the sanctuary and one window had blown open, and it was Basil's. I had never seen one of those windows open before."

A welcome presence in the Hemingway household, Basil has never been disruptive or frightening. "She's very calm. Nothing is ever moved around," Kathy said. "I believe she just wants to make sure everything is okay."

Basil Hemingway, who departed life in the early years of this century, will always belong to quiet, Victorian Andrews. Along with the gracefully turreted, gabled, and gingerbread-trimmed houses of that era, she is a cherished gem of a bygone age.

Hemingway House is located on Rosemary Avenue in Andrews, which is 18 miles west of Georgetown.

Lucas Bay

Of the many apparitions associated with the War Between the States, perhaps the most elusive is the Lucas Bay light. Seen with eerie clarity as far back as many of Lucas Bay's oldest residents can remember, the light has long been a source of mystery.

During the Civil War, many Georgetonians feared that General William T. Sherman's troops would burn their city. As early as 1862, Federal gunboats began patrolling the harbor, causing much distress in the town and the surrounding countryside.

Union troops, having found out who the major planters and

most avid advocates of secession were, soon discovered the location of the plantation homes belonging to these individuals and began harassing them there. Many planters moved their families and slaves inland, renting or buying farms for the duration of the war in Clarendon County, in Camden, or near Columbia or Spartanburg.

Local officials, fearing the destruction of town and county documents, made hasty plans to move the Georgetown County records to the interior of South Carolina for safekeeping. Inland towns, they felt, were less apt to feel the wrath of Union troops than was Georgetown, a key Southern port.

On April 22, 1862, probate judge Eleazer Waterman was ordered by a local committee to pack up all his records so they could be sent to the town of Chesterfield. When Chesterfield was reduced to ashes by Federal troops, so were most of Georgetown County's records prior to the war. Moving the records, it turned out, was a well-intentioned mistake.

While the removal of the county records to Chesterfield is Georgetown County's best-known error of judgement in the face of the Northern invasion, other well-intentioned plans had more tragic consequences. Such was the case in Lucas Bay.

As the Civil War closed and General Sherman's troops began their fifty-mile-wide swath of burning and destruction, word arrived in Georgetown that Atlanta was in ruins. It stood to reason that Georgetown, a closely guarded seaport surrounded by the homes of many secessionists, slave owners, and planters, would be included in the devastation.

Lucas Bay—located twenty-five miles northwest of Georgetown just across the Great Pee Dee River, which flows across the county line—was considered in grave danger. The tiny community lay beside the booming river town of Bucksport, whose shipping and milling facilities would surely be targets. The people of Lucas Bay prepared for a fiery Federal onslaught.

Many homesteads and plantations were occupied only by women, as the men were still in the Confederate military. As the news that General Sherman was marching from Georgia into South Carolina filled hearts with dread, many women sewed precious jewelry and other small valuables into their corsets and skirt hems. They hid larger heirlooms in mattresses or secretly, hurriedly buried them deep in the woods.

Late one afternoon, hoping to keep her infant child safe from Sherman's troops while helping her family defend its home, a desperate Lucas Bay mother hid the slumbering baby under a nearby bridge that led over a canal that fed a rice field.

As darkness began to fall, a violent storm erupted with crackling lightning and earth-shaking thunder rivaling the fierceness of Sherman's men. Realizing that the rice field was already flooded and that the rain would raise the canal to the bottom of the bridge in no time, the young mother slipped away and raced to rescue her child. Reaching the scene, she held her lantern high to see across the canal to where she had hidden the child. Upon glimpsing her baby, she caught her breath in both relief and fear: the infant was as she had left it, but the swollen canal was lapping just below where it was nestled.

Nearly blinded by driving rain and sharp pellets of hail, she ran across the bridge, too fearful for her child to care about the slippery wood beneath her feet. As she reached the other side and made to dash underneath the bridge to where the child lay, she lost her footing and fell, striking her head on one of the timbers supporting the bridge. Knocked unconscious, she fell headlong into the canal and was swept away, soon followed by her infant child.

———

As the years went by and the tragedy of the young mother and her baby slipped into the past, a mysterious light began to appear near where the unfortunate pair died.

According to Lucas Bay residents who have seen it, the phenomenon begins on the bridge on unpaved Lucas Bay Road. It first appears as a tiny, moving red glow similar to someone walking in the dark smoking a cigarette. The light—generally thought to be that of the young mother's lantern—steadily increases in size as it gets closer, then disappears.

One resident took her children to look for the light about nine o'clock one evening. It appeared near the bridge, tiny and bright, then gradually increased in size as it neared the car where she and her children sat, only to disappear in front of the vehicle. The light was so vivid and frightening that the family never went looking for it again.

Another resident and his brother were walking along Lucas Bay Road in the darkness when they saw the light floating above the treetops, coming slowly toward them. The two men hastily made a bet as to which one of them could stand in the road longer as the light approached. Though they were determined to hold their ground, so eerie was the slow-moving light as it came nearer that neither man won the bet—they fled simultaneously!

Older residents who have known of the light their entire lives recall that sightings were more frequent in the days before regular automobile traffic. Walking through Lucas Bay at dusk without the distraction of other lights, residents frequently observed the mysterious phenomenon. Rainy nights just before or just after dark, Lucas Bay residents agree, have always been the most likely times to see the eerie light, which is sometimes accompanied by the sound of a child's wailing.

As with most ghostly occurrences, the Lucas Bay light is seen by some individuals but not others. Some longtime residents have grown so used to seeing the phantom light that they take it for granted. Other older residents have never seen it.

Long a Lucas Bay tradition, the light has been a source of fearful delight to many a child growing up in the community. One resident recalled that on Thanksgiving night, horse-drawn wagons would collect local children to go and look for the light.

Another resident, now long dead, took the phenomenon very seriously, but for a different reason from anyone else. He believed that the light, which he saw regularly, showed the burial spot of a treasure. He claimed it was the ghost of a woman who had lived on the other side of Lucas Bay. Prior to her death, she had dressed all in black and had been feared as a witch. This treasure-hunting resident dug and searched in the vicinity where he saw the light, believing it would lead him to the treasure the witch woman had buried before she died. What he finally found was an empty hole he was sure had contained the treasure, which someone else had gotten to first. After this, he never saw the light again. In his view, the light no longer had a reason to appear, since the treasure had been found.

According to local people, the Lucas Bay light has not been seen in ten or fifteen years. The area it once frequented is traversed by two to three miles of unpaved road lined by forest. Sun-dappled and pristine by day, it is downright eerie at night. Not so much as a single dwelling is to be seen anywhere along this stretch of road. Even today, the Lucas Bay bridge is decidedly spooky, particularly on dark, rainy evenings.

Will the long-dead Lucas Bay mother return again someday for her child, lantern in hand?

Lucas Bay is 25 miles northwest of Georgetown off U.S. 701, just past the Great Pee Dee River bridge.

Bucksville and
Bucksport

When Captain Henry Buck founded Bucksville on the banks of the Waccamaw River in 1825, he planned for it to become a thriving community based on lumbering and shipping. His dream soon became a vibrant, lucrative reality.

What Buck did not consider, however, was a long-ago, thousand-mile curse that, according to some, came back to haunt his thriving community and cause its demise.

Beginning in the early 1700s, lumber left Georgetown Harbor

destined for distant ports. But it was not a large part of Georgetown's export trade until Captain Henry Buck constructed three lumbermills on the upper Waccamaw River. Soon, lumber became one of the town's greatest export commodities.

In the days before steam-powered maritime transport, sailing ships were a principal means of trade. The Northern shipyards where most American vessels were built needed great supplies of lumber to construct these graceful vessels. Captain Henry Buck was determined to supply that need.

When Buck settled on the Waccamaw River, he built a lovely home and constructed a lumbermill beside it. Milling and shipping lumber and shingles cut from the low country forests was so lucrative that he soon built a second Bucksville mill several miles downstream. A third lumbermill, referred to as "the lower mill," was opened downriver from the first two and christened Bucksport, after the town of the same name in Maine.

As these steam-powered sawmills prospered, the town of Bucksville grew. Ships destined for New England, New York, and the West Indies left Bucksville loaded with lumber. On their way south to Bucksville and Bucksport in winter, New England ships used ice for ballast. As these ships off-loaded ballast before taking on their cargo of South Carolina lumber, Captain Henry Buck began selling the ice—a rare commodity on the Waccamaw—from one of the first icehouses in the area.

But ice was just a minor portion of Buck's trade. During a two-year period just prior to 1840, fifty-two ships sailed out of Bucksville. The *Winyah Observer* of November 8, 1845, noted that one sloop, one schooner, and nine brigs were loading lumber at Bucksville. By January 1848, as many as twenty-eight ships at a time were loading there.

The men who came to work in the mills brought families. Soon, Bucksville had schools, churches, hotels, and a post office. At the onset of the Civil War, the town had a population of seven hundred. As the Confederate cannonballs flew toward Fort Sumter in Charleston Harbor, a number of Northern captains engaged in commerce at Bucksville hastily untied their dock lines and sailed north to avoid being caught in the conflict.

After the war, the Bucksville lumber industry did not suffer the hardships of the weak Reconstruction economy, but remained prosperous. A constant stream of three-masted vessels came in off the Atlantic to sail over the sand bar into Georgetown Harbor and make their way up the Waccamaw River to load lumber from Bucksville's three-quarter-mile-long dock. Ports around the world were recipients of the four million feet of cypress shingles and the six million feet of lumber milled and shipped out of Bucksville each year.

After the death of Captain Henry Buck, his son W. L. Buck became responsible for running the mills. In keeping with family tradition, he began a foray into shipbuilding in 1874.

Bucksport, Maine, located beside the dark waters of the Penobscot River, had gained fame as a shipbuilding town in the century since its founding. Bucksville and Bucksport in South Carolina were now set to rival their namesake. Two similar ships were to be constructed simultaneously, one in Bucksport, Maine, and the other in Bucksville, South Carolina. Each town determined that the vessel it constructed would be finer and would be completed in a shorter time and with less money than the other shipyard could manage.

W. L. Buck, master shipwright Elishua Dunbar, Captain Jonathan Nichols, and a crew of 115 riggers, joiners, and marine carpenters began construction of the *Henrietta*, a square-rigged clipper ship. Bucksville on the Waccamaw won by a great margin. The breathtakingly beautiful *Henrietta*, named after Captain Nichols's daughter, was launched from Bucksville, South Carolina, in May 1875, her keel having been laid the previous September. She was 201 feet long and weighed 1,204 tons. She cost approximately $90,000, some $25,000 less than her Northern counterpart.

Two more ships—the schooner *Hattie Buck* and the barque-rigged *Henry Buck*—were built at the Bucksville-Bucksport lumberyards. The area now had another lucrative industry: shipbuilding.

––––––

Bucksville and Bucksport seemed destined to thrive. But this was not to be. Why? According to some, the reason lay generations earlier.

When Captain Henry Buck founded Bucksville on the Waccamaw River in 1825, he was not the first in his family to establish a town. In 1762, Boston native Jonathan Buck had sailed north to settle in Maine. There, on the Penobscot River, he had discovered an excellent site for the shipping of lumber, fish, and other products. He began the town of Bucksport—then called Buckstown—in 1764.

In addition to being founder of the town, Jonathan Buck had the honor of being elected magistrate. One of those pronounced guilty under his jurisdiction was a woman believed to be a witch. Buck sentenced her to a severe whipping. Just as he finished announcing her fate, the woman laid a curse on him. Never again, she swore, would a Buck stand in judgment over his own town as Judge Buck did here. Any attempt, anywhere, to create another such township would eventually fail, she decreed. The sign of the curse, she said, would follow him to his grave and appear in plain view on his tombstone as proof the curse had truly been cast. This sign would be a likeness of her leg with whip slashes upon its.

According to many local residents, the witch's punishment was much worse. Rather than being merely thrashed, they say, she was burned, and her foot dropped off into the execution fire.

Judge Buck died on March 18, 1795. After his death, the sign appeared on his tombstone, just as the witch had predicted. Some of the judge's descendants voiced their indignation at what they considered a besmirching of his memory. Nevertheless, the unmistakable foot and leg of the witch mark the judge's tall, graceful monument above his grave site in Bucksport, Maine, to this day.

And the curse? Some say it was borne out a thousand miles away and a hundred years later in the lumbermills of Bucksville and Bucksport in South Carolina, which declined after less than a century of prosperity. Many towns have suffered hardships that resulted in economic depression, neglect, and diminished population. But none has ever thrived so vigorously and then disappeared so completely as Bucksville. It is truly a town that vanished.

Although applications were submitted more than once for the busy port of Bucksville to be made a port of entry, Congress refused each time, first suggesting Bucksville as a port of delivery instead. Upon the second application, the customs collector of Georgetown told the secretary of the treasury that to allow Bucksville to become a port of entry would be to legitimize what was one of the best places for smuggling in the United States.

And the fine, cost-efficient construction that produced the *Henrietta* was a feat never to be repeated. The pride of her home port, the *Henrietta* never returned to Bucksville. She drew too much water to cross back over the sand bar at the entrance to Georgetown Harbor even at high tide. Her maiden crossing had been so treacherous and time-consuming that she had barely made it seaward across the twelve feet of water over the bar. Her captain dared not take her back across for fear that she would founder, as had many large or unwary ships over the years. A fast, durable ship that should have plied the seas for many decades, the *Henrietta* was lost in Japan in 1894 during a typhoon, far from the home port she never revisited.

The other two ships built in Bucksville, the *Hattie Buck* and the *Henry Buck*, were as well designed as the *Henrietta*. Unlike the

Henrietta, they had a shallow-enough draft to pass over the Georgetown bar. Still, despite these shipbuilding successes, W. L. Buck discontinued his manufacture of sailing vessels. His best customers, the Northern shipyards that purchased his lumber, disliked the competition. They simply told Buck to stop building ships or they would stop purchasing lumber from him.

The Bucksville and Bucksport lumbermills continued to prosper into the early twentieth century. Then, suddenly, the combined effects of a great fire and the Depression ended the town of Bucksville altogether. Schools, hotels, churches, post office, citizens—everything and everyone disappeared. Was this the fulfillment of the Maine witch's curse?

Today, the picturesque harbor at Bucksport is a prerequisite stopover for many finely appointed sailing vessels and yachts on the Intracoastal Waterway. With its beautifully appointed marina and restaurant, it is a spot where grateful travelers take rest and repast. Except for the abandoned house where the owner of the lumbermill once lived and a huge building made entirely of the cypress shingles the local mills were famous for, there is little to attest that a mill ever stood at Bucksport.

Little remains of Bucksville save two nineteenth-century structures built by Captain Henry Buck. One is the well-kept Buck plantation house, complete with former slave cabins. The other is Hebron Methodist Church, constructed in 1848 and now listed on the National Register of Historic Places.

And what of the lumbermills that began the town? All that

remains are two chimneys, each standing alone where a thriving mill once bustled around it. The chimney of the earliest mill is near the Buck plantation house. The other chimney is a little farther downriver. Once part of a multilevel structure recognized as the largest mill in South Carolina, it towers seventy-five feet above the ground.

The mills are as completely forgotten as the long-lost railroad tracks that once carried millions of feet of lumber to the Bucksville docks. The booming lumber trade and the shipbuilding industry, both of which should have reached legendary proportions, are lost to the past, perhaps casualties of a witch's curse placed long ago and far away.

Bucksville and Bucksport are, respectively, 37 and 34 miles north of Georgetown. Visitors will reach their sites several miles after crossing the Great Pee Dee River on U.S. 701.

Wedgefield

The Revolutionary War and the British occupation of Georgetown left changes on the port town and surrounding Prince George Parish. A number of lovely homes belonging to those who supported the Patriot cause were burned during the siege. Most Patriot families, ordered to evacuate their houses to make room for the British military, were later able to move back home. Plantations resumed regular operations. Property belonging to those loyal to Britain was confiscated. Most of these landowners petitioned for pardon, promised loyalty to the new American government, and were given their property back.

Changes of an ethereal nature took place, too. One member of the British military who lost his life in Prince George Parish remains here to this day, haunting the scene of his last earthly hours.

———————

During the early years of the American Revolution, Georgetown was safe from British attack. Although word came in the spring of 1776 that the English planned to attack Charles Town, only sixty miles south, Georgetown County was unfriendly to any kind of military maneuvers save guerrilla warfare, thanks to its five rivers and its miles of swamps. When the British attacked Fort Moultrie, just north of Charles Town Harbor, that July 28, two companies of Georgetown volunteers marched down to help save the fort.

Georgetown felt few effects of the war until May 12, 1780, when Charles Town finally fell. Soon, Georgetown was besieged by sea and by land. As the closest port to Charles Town, it became a focal point of British naval attention. British sailors were dispatched up the rivers on armed barges to raid the plantations. The Sixty-third Royal Regiment pillaged by land. British naval vessels anchored in the harbor. The men and horses of the cavalry took quarters in the township. For their stable, the king's men used the centrally located parish church of Prince George Winyah, quartering their horses in the box pews of the sanctuary itself. Even though Prince George Winyah was an Anglican church, the Crown's men caused fire damage to the interior of the structure sometime during their occupation.

Although most Georgetonians were Patriots, a number of citizens wished to continue under British rule. Those who were loyal to the king were scornfully called "Tories" by their Patriot neighbors.

One Front Street resident who sympathized with the British was the subject of much discussion among his neighbors, who wanted to punish but not harm him. The Patriots agreed among themselves not to sell the man any salt. Although this may seem a minor matter, the lack of salt caused him and his family discomfort, aggravation, and hardship, for without salt, they could not cure meat. Fish, fowl, and red meat, whether hunted or bought, had to be eaten at once or thrown away.

Several loyal British subjects living in Georgetown opened their townhouses to the military representatives of the Crown, gladly hosting officers. Patriots, however, were not requested to host the enemy. They were simply told to evacuate so the British could use their homes.

As the occupation continued, more and more temporary housing was needed for English troops and their Patriot prisoners. When space in even outbuildings and sheds in the township became scarce, the British began using some of the outlying plantation homes. Wedgefield Plantation, several miles north of Georgetown on the Black River, was chosen as a suitable place to sequester Patriot prisoners and allow injured British soldiers to recuperate.

One of the prisoners, an elderly gentleman, was particularly important to the British. The father of one of General Francis

Marion's officers, he held vast knowledge of the Patriot general's swamp and island hideaways.

A native of the South Carolina low country, General Marion, aptly nicknamed "the Swamp Fox," easily navigated the endless swamps, creeks, and rivers of his boyhood home, constantly leaving pursuing British troops lost or stranded. But the capture of the father of one of his officers was a possible security breach. Though wise and trustworthy, the old gentleman was becoming confused in his advanced age. General Marion feared that the elderly fellow, fiercely loyal to the Patriot cause, would unwittingly divulge precious secrets to the enemy.

Of course, that was exactly what the British hoped. They also knew that General Marion, who always seemed to anticipate their plans, was fully aware of the situation and had placed top priority on retrieving the prisoner. For this reason, the British assigned twenty troops to guard the elderly gentleman at Wedgefield.

The owner of Wedgefield also possessed homes in Georgetown and Charles Town, a store in Charles Town, and a merchant ship that made regular runs between the two cities. A shrewd businessman, he had decided early in the war not to choose sides, for conducting business with both the British and the Americans was much more profitable than being loyal to one side or the other. During the time the British occupied Charles Town but not Georgetown, a number of Georgetown merchants traded lucratively with the British, supplying them with rice, tobacco, and clothing. The Patriot militia disapproved of but did not forbid this trade. However, as the war progressed and the British took command of Georgetown, questions of loyalty became increasingly important, and merchants were pressed into declaring their loyalty to the Patriots or the Crown.

Wedgefield's owner did not have to debate for long. As the greater portion of his business depended on the British, he chose to support the Crown. From then on, he was publicly known as a Tory. But unbeknownst to the British and even to her own father, the daughter of Wedgefield's owner remained secretly loyal to the Patriot cause.

When not in Charles Town, the owner and his daughter divided their time between Wedgefield and their Georgetown townhouse, where British troops were also quartered. Quite often, the ever-wary daughter heard military information uttered by English soldiers. It never occurred to the British that, in quarters provided by a loyal subject of the Crown, a Patriot spy was in their midst.

The formal garden of the townhouse was near the churchyard of Prince George Winyah, where the daughter secretly delivered information to the Patriots of Georgetown. She would slip into a lonely corner of the churchyard under cover of darkness and leave messages containing the information she had gleaned from listening to conversations in her father's townhouse and at Wedgefield. In the same designated spot among the crypts and tombstones, communiqués detailing needed information would be left for her by General Marion's men.

It was through the daughter's careful eavesdropping that

Marion discovered where the elderly gentleman was being held. Knowing that the old fellow might suffer confusion at any time and release Patriot information to his captors, Marion gave the daughter his blessing to execute an ingenious plan to retrieve the elderly gentleman.

Thus, the daughter arranged with a few Tory ladies to present an evening's entertainment for the British troops quartered at Mansfield Plantation, just north of Wedgefield. Of course, the daughter insisted that the guards at lonely Wedgefield be included. Her plan for retrieving the elderly gentleman hinged on the guards' attendance.

Just as she and General Marion hoped, the Wedgefield guards were delighted at the opportunity to spend part of an evening at the Mansfield gala. As the sun was sinking, all the Wedgefield guards—save one man who stayed to watch the prisoners—mounted their horses and cantered down the long plantation avenue on their way to a festive evening.

As darkness descended over the Black River, which flows behind both Wedgefield and Mansfield, a band of General Marion's men galloped their horses up the Wedgefield avenue toward the spacious two-and-a-half-story home. The sentry, expecting a quiet, lonely evening, was surprised to hear hoofbeats. Assuming that British troops from Georgetown were riding out to attend the entertainment at Mansfield, he hurried down the steps of the manor to hail them and direct them next door to Mansfield. The horsemen reined in close to the house just as the sentry reached the bottom of the steps. They were nearly hovering over him as he saw with a shock that these were Patriot troops.

Not one to surrender, he instantly had his pistol in hand and aimed it at the rider closest to him. The Patriot rider drew a bead on the sentry at the same instant. Both men fired. Both missed their target. As the fire from the two barrels flashed in the near-darkness, the twin bursts of flame illuminated the razor edge of a swiftly drawn saber sweeping through the air. Wielded by one of the Patriot riders instinctively protecting his fellow soldier, the blade found its mark. As the smoke from the discharged pistols rose, the head of the British sentry fell to the ground. The few seconds of violence over, the Patriot party watched in shock as the headless sentry staggered about for several agonizing moments before collapsing lifeless on the ground.

With only one sentry to contend with, the Patriots had hoped to complete their mission without a struggle, much less a fatality. They completed their business in stony near-silence, quickly freeing the elderly gentleman and several other Patriot prisoners. They also took a number of wounded British soldiers who had been convalescing at Wedgefield.

The unfortunate sentry was buried in the Wedgefield garden. When British occupation was finally behind them, Georgetonians settled down to repairing damage from the siege. Though the town and the surrounding countryside were now free from unrest, all was not peaceful at Wedgefield Plantation.

During the years following the war, gunfire and hoofbeats were often heard just after dark in the vicinity of the manor house, though there was no apparent source. A shadowy, pistol-brandishing figure in British military garb began to appear early on moonlit evenings, moving rapidly about the porch and steps of the house. What looked to be the same figure—only headless—was often glimpsed walking erratically near the base of the steps, apparently searching for something. Servants whispered that this terrible sight was the ghost of the British sentry looking for his missing head.

A century and a half later, during the 1930s, the old Wedgefield manor house was torn down and replaced by the present mansion. Georgetonians familiar with the ghost who once paced the porch there noted that the apparition was glimpsed less often after the old house was gone.

But he still appears on rare occasions on the plantation avenue at Wedgefield near the site of the long-gone steps where his life so suddenly ended. His appearances are heralded by the sounds of hoofbeats and gunfire, which represent the confusion of his final seconds on earth and the swiftness of his demise.

Sometimes, he is seen, head intact, in the vicinity of the old Wedgefield garden, wandering forlornly above his final resting place, where his body was united with its severed head once more.

Wedgefield Plantation is located just north of Georgetown on U.S. 701.

Bolem House

Everyone does not have the ability to see ghosts. Someone with this gift is often the only person among several in a room or a house who can sense a presence not of this world. Such was the case during the 1993 Christmas season at Bolem House, a home with a close connection to Georgetown's early nautical history.

Georgetown was laid out in 1729. At the insistence of South Carolina's newly appointed colonial leader, Royal Governor Robert Johnson, the township was made a port of entry in 1731. Georgetown Harbor soon became busy with shipping.

One of the oldest homes in Georgetown, Bolem House was built very near the street in the 1730s. With its generous bay windows and its nine-foot double doors opening into rooms with ten-foot ceilings, it is airy and sunlit. The paneled sections above several doors show the fine detailing that went into the home's construction. Charming and comfortable, with that certain ambiance that only well-cared-for centuries-old homes boast, Bolem House still has much of its original flooring, cut from the full cross-sections of great trees. Those floors have absorbed many a footstep over the last 260 years.

Records show that in the mid-nineteenth century, Bolem House came into the hands of David and Sarah Sperry of Charleston, who sold it to Edward T. Henning in 1874. The house then belonged to Simons E. Lucas of North Carolina, then to William T. Upgrove of Georgetown, then to O. B. Skinner, then to Confederate veteran Gilbert Johnson, who died here in 1925. Following Johnson's death, his sister-in-law sold Bolem House to T. Cordes Lucas of South Santee. Leta Cribb moved in with her family some years later and has been here ever since.

But what of the years prior to the mid-1800s? The house was obviously constructed when Prince Street was much narrower. The sidewalk had to be built around the home's double piazzas, making it the only house in Georgetown with piazzas literally at the sidewalk.

The mystery began to be unraveled during the early 1970s, when Leta's husband, Howard, did major gardening excavation behind the house and unearthed artifacts from the home's early days. In addition to finding a long-buried cistern, used by early owners to keep perishables cool and fresh, he unearthed an unusually large cache of old bottles. Howard had discovered evidence of an eighteenth-century tavern!

His discoveries inspired him to undertake extensive research about the origin of the house. In the archives of the Charleston Library Society, he uncovered previously unrealized facts in microfilm issues of the *South Carolina Gazette*. Notices in the *Gazette* in 1734 and 1735 announced meetings at the establishment of Thomas Bolem, during which lot owners in the township could take up property discrepancies with the town trustees.

Better yet was a 1737 legal notice concerning the estate of the recently deceased owner: "All persons indebted to the estate of Thomas Bolem . . . are hereby desired to pay their respective debts to Sussannah Bolem, Executrix or the Reverend John Fordyce, Executor of the said estate within a month's time, to whom those that have any demands may apply for payment. The house where the said Bolem deceased, lately kept Tavern in Georgetown being well accustom'd and provided with all conveniences, is to be LETT and two lots in George Town to be SOLD."

The tavern's location—the *Gazette* described it as being "500 feet from the George Town River [now the Sampit River] on Princes Street"—made it a popular spot with the thirsty sailors from the many ships that tied up at the wharves.

The sailors found Thomas Bolem's tavern to be a home away from home, where they could wind down from their rigorous shipboard duties. In fact, at least one of them was so fond of the place that he was drawn back more than two and a half centuries later to enjoy some age-old Christmas cheer.

———

The ghostly opening and closing of firmly latched doors has

long been taken for granted in Bolem House. Having lived there since 1938, Leta simply accepts it.

Christmas 1993, however, brought the house's quiet ghost briefly into focus. One of the guests at Leta's tree trimming told his son afterwards of encountering an old-fashioned man at Bolem House, a man who, it turned out, had not been visible to anyone else.

The son related the story thus: "Daddy was helping Leta decorate the Christmas tree and went into the kitchen for something and encountered a very old man in an old-time sailor's outfit, and he appeared to have no teeth. The man wandered around the kitchen, then into a hallway, never saying anything and looking somewhat displaced. On mentioning the guest to my mother, Leta, and the few other guests, no one had seen him, nor was Leta expecting any other guests. She did later, however, say that the house is haunted."

So it was that one of Thomas Bolem's customers returned to his old stomping ground. Habitually heard but seen only this once, the ghost of the eighteenth-century sailor is apparently a soft touch for holiday cheer and the remembrance of Christmases past.

Bolem House is located at 719 Prince Street in Georgetown's historic district.

The
Rice Museum

A favorite subject of local and visiting artists, the picturesque bell and clock tower under which the Rice Museum resides is the landmark most often associated with Georgetown. This Greek Revival structure, believed to have been copied from the town hall and clock building in Keswick, England, was formerly a slave market.

Although the portion of the museum containing detailed dioramas of rice and indigo production is underneath the Town Clock in the Old Market Building, the Rice Museum consists of both this structure and the antebellum Kaminski Building next door.

A feeling of the past prevails at these two venerable structures. Those gifted with the ability to sense the presence of ghosts, however, may experience a more ethereal awareness.

———

The first town market was built on what is now the site of the Old Market Building in 1788. This wooden market was badly damaged by a hurricane in 1822. In 1841, as a severe fire was decimating the Front Street businesses between Queen and Screven Streets, the storm-damaged market was torn down as a firebreak. It was reconstructed of brick in 1842. Three years later, the celebrated bell and clock tower was added. In fact, most Georgetonians refer to the Old Market Building as the "Town Clock."

Union ships landed on the riverfront behind the Town Clock when they began patrolling the Georgetown waterfront. Near the close of the Civil War, the Old Market Building was where surrender papers were signed by the town council and turned over to Federal officers, as Union-occupied Georgetown yielded to the victorious North. The end of slavery in Georgetown was thus finalized where slaves were once sold. This abrupt end to the practice of slavery heralded the beginning of the end of the Georgetown rice culture.

Until recent decades, this historic structure housed Georgetown's town hall on its second story and the police department on its ground floor.

On the southeastern side of the Old Market Building stands the Kaminski Building. Built in 1842, the same year as the Old

Market Building, it replaced a two-story warehouse destroyed in the fire of 1841. By the late 1850s, the Kaminski Building was Stephen W. Rouquie's hardware and dry-goods emporium. During Rouquie's ownership, a cast-iron front designed by New York architect Daniel Badger was built into the facade.

Near the close of the Civil War, Rouquie allowed Thomas Daggett, the Confederate captain of coastal defenses from Little River to Georgetown, to use the upper story of his store to build a mine. This mine was used by Captain Daggett to destroy the *Harvest Moon*, the only Union flagship sunk during the war.

In 1869, Rouquie sold the building to Heiman Kaminski, an amiable, ambitious thirty-year-old Confederate veteran who had been renting the structure and operating a store there for two years. In 1878, Kaminski renovated the building with major architectural work that included the addition of a third floor, a three-story light well, a skylight, a spacious rear section, and Italianate detailing on the facade.

At the northwestern side of the Rice Museum lies the immaculately tended garden of the Lowcountry Herb Society. All of the medicinal and culinary herbs grown here are indigenous to the area or have, like indigo, been cultivated here since colonial times. The propagation of herbs creates an atmosphere befitting the museum above, where a cornucopia of artifacts depicts a heritage based on the cultivation of fertile soil.

In 1970, the city of Georgetown sold the Old Market Building to the Georgetown Historical Society. That May, the society unveiled the Rice Museum as part of the celebration of South Carolina's tricentennial.

Ever since then, the Old Market Building has housed the museum's extensive collection of rice- and indigo-cultivation artifacts. Dioramas detail the process of eighteenth- and nineteenth-century rice propagation, from sowing to harvest to shipping. The dioramas also tell about the slave labor that made it possible for the Georgetown-area coast to yield nearly half the nation's rice during the 1840s.

The Kaminski Building houses the Rice Museum Annex and the museum's Prevost Art Gallery. Located on the lower floor, the Prevost Art Gallery hosts an ever-changing display of original works by low country artists. In the forward area of the gallery is a shop where myriad local treasures—including books, baskets, pottery, and jewelry—are sold. Beautifully produced by the Rice Museum's director, James Fitch, the documentary films shown in the gallery focus on important but often overlooked aspects of Georgetown's history.

The upper story of the Rice Museum Annex houses the Browns Ferry Vessel, believed to be the oldest colonial merchant vessel in the Western Hemisphere. Sunk in the Black River near Browns Ferry in the 1740s, it was lowered into the museum's third story by crane in June 1992, after extensive stabilization and salvage work had been done. The museum's roof was temporarily removed to facilitate placement of the vessel.

With so much having taken place here over the past two

centuries, it is no wonder that Sarah Johnson, who works in the Rice Museum, is often aware of the presence of a ghostly overseer watching her as she works, as if to check the quality of her performance.

It is also not surprising that ghostly footsteps are heard upstairs over the Prevost Art Gallery in the Kaminski Building. Eileen Weaver, who works in the gallery, occasionally hears the unmistakable gait of an individual with a peg leg moving across the floor above her to the Front Street window. James Fitch has also heard the ghostly footsteps.

Because of the value of the Browns Ferry Vessel, preserved upstairs, anyone going above the first floor of the building is carefully monitored. The museum staff therefore knows when no one—no one human, at least—is up there. Only when the second and third floors are empty are the footsteps heard.

Weaver has had other ghostly experiences in the museum as well. Blessed since childhood with the rare ability to see and hear ghosts, she could no doubt fill a volume with the ghostly appearances she has witnessed.

Several times, she has been surprised by the figure of a lady from another century in the gallery. On each occasion, she has seen the lady pacing back and forth in front of a plantation sideboard built in 1845 and donated to the museum in 1985. Described by Weaver as an old black woman wearing a black dress with a ruffled collar, the lady is very possessive of the sideboard. Her motions seem to silently say, "It's mine, it's mine," before she simply evaporates.

The sideboard is extremely difficult to open. When necessary, James Fitch opens it by using force, prying the doors loose with a key. Yet sometimes, the doors are simply flung open during museum hours when no one is anywhere near the sideboard.

Whoever the lady is, she does not have to force the doors, but simply opens them with no prying—as she has perhaps been doing for a century and a half. But why is this mysterious, ghostly lady so attached to the sideboard?

Weaver, who has researched some of the ghosts she has seen, believes this lady is the ghost of a slave from the plantation where the sideboard was built—a house slave, in fact, who had a great personal interest in the sideboard. "You know, the slaves built so much of the furniture at these plantations," Weaver said. "And it is a historic fact that they almost always put a secret compartment in each piece they built."

Whether a secret compartment was found and removed long ago or still lies untouched deep inside the labyrinth of the sideboard is known only by the ethereal lady who lingers possessively at the relic's doors and opens them with an ease no one else can duplicate.

The Rice Museum is located on the Georgetown waterfront at the intersection of Front and Screven Streets.

Keith House

While the lineage of many houses in Georgetown's historic district can be traced back to the deed of the first owner, the line of title for some homes does not begin there. In a number of cases, the record of original ownership was apparently lost or not documented at all until the house was subsequently sold or included in the estate of a later owner.

Such is the case with Keith House, which has no record of deed or documented historic mention until 1855, when it was sold by Paul Trapier Keith and John Alexander Keith. The years before the Keiths sold the house are, and probably always will be, a mystery.

Whoever constructed this elegant, two-story, hip-roofed home dated it with four-panel doors, plaster ceiling medallions in one of the downstairs formal rooms, and six-over-six sash windows with narrow muntins, all indicative of construction around 1825. Great care was also taken in the placement of the dentil molding adorning the cornice and mantel of another formal room downstairs.

Keith House has been home to numerous families since its construction. One woman fondly remembers her girlhood in the spacious old home. Her father bought and remodeled it, adding a large rear section where his children could entertain their friends.

The legend of Keith House stands out vividly in this woman's memory, for it is a story not easily forgotten. Although the legend is an integral part of the Georgetown tradition, the passing of time has obscured the name of the long-ago lady of the house, an antebellum gentlewoman with an eerie style of clairvoyance. Time, however, cannot dim the spine-tingling nature of the story.

Before the Civil War, Keith House was the home of an extraordinarily lovely young belle. Later in her life, after she had grown into a handsome elderly woman, she was plagued by painful arthritis in her hands and became overly self-conscious about their gnarled condition. Long a widow, she had worn only black clothing since her beloved husband's passing. Now, she took to wearing black mittens at all times, so no one could see her misshapen fingers.

More important, the lady began making astounding and eerily accurate predictions of unexpected deaths among family and friends. Her clairvoyance earned the unwavering awe of household servants, who believed she was a witch.

After the lady's death, her reputation for macabre prediction only gained momentum. She would, servants whispered, materialize from the small room under the stairwell and, dressed in her customary black clothing and black mittens, appear to family members preceding a death among them. Household servants began avoiding the room under the stairwell. After a fateful glimpse of the ghostly, black-draped figure, more than one of them was left to agonize over whose mortal hours were growing short. Family members, too, dreaded the appearance of their clairvoyant kinswoman.

In life, her predictions of impending death had been both accurate and timely; she had often named both the unfortunate individual and the hour of his or her demise. After her death, the lady's ghostly, voiceless, ephemeral manifestation was always a harbinger of death. Only now, the identity of the person soon to die was a mystery, leaving the household wondering which among them it would be.

The lady who became a ghostly portent of doom has not been seen in many years. This may be only because no relative of hers has lived in her old home since the years immediately following her death, when she would come forth from beneath the stairs to issue uncanny messages of fate.

Keith House is located at
1012 Front Street in Georgetown.

Hags
and Plat-Eyes

Though most Georgetown
hauntings involve ghosts, which are not harmful and are not to
be feared, there are shadowy beings that must be stringently
avoided. Often mentioned in the same breath, hags and plat-
eyes are not so much like each other as they are different from
ghosts.

Ghosts are not baneful and tend to predictably repeat the same
actions over and over, occasionally with benevolence but usually
with complete indifference to human activities. Hags and plat-
eyes are quite the opposite. They are malevolent, sometimes un-
predictable creatures that relish interaction with people.

In Georgetown's historic district, it is not uncommon to see the ceilings of the verandas of old houses painted robin's-egg blue. The owners of many houses with double piazzas paint each piazza ceiling this shade as well. The effect is striking, because the ceilings are the lone blue adornment on these structures, not matching the principal or trim colors. There is no reason for the blue ceilings except that they are a time-honored means of warding off hags and plat-eyes. For the same reason, many cottages in the Georgetown County countryside are trimmed in bright blue or are painted blue in their entirety.

The tradition of using blue paint as protection is only one part of the extensive lore that has grown up around hags and plat-eyes. The list of strange and inventive means that people have devised for guarding against them is long indeed.

The plat-eye has long been feared for its aggressiveness. Never without mischievous intentions, it haunts lonely places such as swamps, low-lying areas, and old rice fields, preying on travelers and passersby who chance to cross its path. The plat-eye has front teeth but no back teeth and has long been associated with the time of the new moon.

Described in the John Bennett Papers—housed in the archives of the South Carolina Historical Society—as the "projected spirit of malevolent humanity," the plat-eye rarely leaves the swirling mist in which it lurks except to chase an intended victim. "The mist which it rises from," reads the archives' description, "is usually a steaming rice field." Many people who lived on Prospect Hill Plantation from the mid-nineteenth century to the early twentieth century were recorded as being "deathly afraid" of plat-eyes.

In its natural form, the plat-eye has one large eye, round and white like a plate, from which it takes its name. This creature possesses broad powers of transformation. It usually takes the form of a small, fiery-eyed dog that grows larger with every passing second, but it has also been known to appear as a horse or some other creature. In one case, a murdered husband leaped out of his coffin in the shape of a frog, shifted into his human form, and went back into the coffin.

Plat-eyes are to be avoided at all costs. Contact can usually be averted by keeping clear of swampy, low-lying areas and abandoned rice fields at night.

Hags, however, are not so easily eluded. Rather than keeping to outlying swampy areas, they seek out the homes of unsuspecting humans.

During the day, the hag appears to be a normal human female. After shedding its skin at night, however, it reveals itself to be a creature half vapor and half liquid. Relieved of its skin, the hag flits through the night, its form barely visible, glimmering in the wind as it hurries on its way to "ride" a victim. In its diaphanous form, it freely slips through even the tiniest of keyholes into the securest of homes to prey on the slumbering victim of its choice.

After gaining access to a dwelling, the hag visits night after night, creeping into the victim's room to ride him or her. Unaware of the hag's visits, the victim awakens unrefreshed and tired even after a full night's sleep. Hags have been known to cause nightmares in men and convulsions in children. They have no preference in victims and are just as likely to prey on children and women as on the elderly and men.

The symptoms of being ridden by a hag are described in the archives of the South Carolina Historical Society: "From these assaults the victim wakes enervated, exhausted, dizzy, depressed, unconscious of any excess but actually suffering from a morbid condition." Hags bring "dire consequences upon the victim's body and mind." Much has been recorded concerning these stealthy creatures who "divest themselves of human skins and flit through the night in a corporeal but fluid condition."

Unaware that a hag has been wearing him out every night, the victim often wastes time seeking a medical reason for waking up tired each morning. Soon, most victims realize their fatigue has no medical basis and begin to suspect the unsettling truth.

Fortunately, the hag-ridden are only disturbed at night. Once an individual suspects he is the victim of a hag, he can devote his waking hours to keeping the creature out of his home.

The ways of deterring a hag are many and diverse but fall into three basic categories: barring the hag's entry, confusing the hag, and catching the hag.

Barring a hag's entry is said to be prudent even if one's home has yet to be violated, since a hag may come along at any time. In order to bar entry, it is necessary to secure every opening the hag might go through. In their half-vapor, half-liquid state, hags are particularly fond of tiny entryways like keyholes and the spaces underneath doors, which are often overlooked by humans as means of entry.

If a hag slides underneath a door or slips through a keyhole, a handful of mustard seeds scattered on the floor will stop it immediately. The hag will be compelled to pick up every tiny seed before it continues through the home to seize its victim. In like manner, a broom propped upside down next to a door will compel a hag to count every straw before it proceeds through the house. A horseshoe hung above a door will ensure that, before it is free to seek its victim, the hag must tread every mile of roadway traveled by the horseshoe.

These methods of forcing a hag to gather, to count, or to traverse many miles are effective precautions, because a hag can only enter a home late at night and must exit before the first light of dawn. These time-consuming tasks will most likely occupy it until it must leave to retrieve its skin.

A shrewd hag, however, may learn to overcome these obstacles or may simply get faster at gathering mustard seeds, counting broom straws, or traversing a horseshoe's miles. Or it may find an opening into a home that no one has thought to protect, thereby avoiding contact with the deterrents.

Since a hag may slip into a home regardless of any precautions taken to bar it, it is best to vigilantly guard innocent sleepers. To keep a hag away once the occupant of a bed has fallen asleep, the person should, upon climbing into bed, place an open Bible or prayer book under his head. After pulling up the covers and getting settled, the person should then lay a flannel skirt across the middle of the bed, positioning it carefully so it does not fall away during the night. In one instance, a flannel skirt slid off before dawn and the waiting hag seized the occupant of the bed.

In addition to these precautions, the person should hang a necklace of alligator teeth and a small piece of asafetida—a protective but highly odoriferous herb—around the neck.

In most cases, a person is free to rest without fear of a hag's visit after taking these measures. But sometimes, the only way to be rid of a hag is to catch it and end its visits permanently. A captured hag must be prevented from returning to its skin before daylight. With no protective skin, it weakens considerably in the light of day and is able to ride a victim no more.

A small, open container of vinegar, spit, and onions hung on the inside of a doorknob has long been considered an excellent hag trap. As recorded in the archives of the South Carolina Historical Society, another time-honored—but more distasteful—way of catching a hag is as follows: "One may set traps with phials with wide open mouths half full of voided waters suspended immediately below the keyhole where the hag slips in."

Should a hag elude these traps, it is up to the victim to wake up and catch it.

Since a hag always departs over the head of a bed, the headboard should be placed against the wall. When the hag is about to leave just before dawn, it will be trapped against the wall. The victim can then, upon waking, seize it.

If a victim wakes during the night and does not see or hear

the hag but rather senses its presence, he should take a three-tine fork and thrust its points into the floor at the side of the bed. This will pin the vaporous hag to the floor, where it will remain until the fork is lifted.

Another method will work only for victims so exhausted from hag-ridden nights that they can fall asleep with a flour sifter on their face and a three-tine fork beneath it. Upon reaching a person who has protected himself thus, the hag is compelled to count every tiny hole in the wire-mesh basket before getting at its prey. During the time the hag is whispering to itself as it painstakingly counts the holes, the victim should be able to wake up—or so the theory goes. The victim should then snatch the flour sifter and the fork off his face and plunge the fork into the wire basket, pinning the hag so it cannot escape. Should the victim be so tired from his nightly ordeals as to not awaken, the fork should effectively pin the hag after it has finished counting and begun to creep through the wire mesh toward its prey.

If catching a hag proves impossible, then finding its skin is an alternative. After doffing its skin in preparation for a nighttime search for mischief, a hag must leave the skin unguarded as it flits about in its half-vapor, half-liquid form. It must then clothe itself in its skin before dawn. A skin that is discovered and treated with salt during the night will cause a hag untold agony when it slips it back on.

In one instance, a lovely woman with very fair, satiny skin was in fact a hag. Unbeknownst to anyone, she shed her skin late every night when her husband was asleep, flitted through the air in her ethereal form to the dwelling of one of her numerous victims, floated through some tiny opening into the home, and rode her poor, slumbering prey to exhaustion until just before dawn. Then she would steal away, fly back home, don her skin, and arrange herself under her bedcovers so her husband would have no inkling that his lovely, gentle wife had been tormenting innocent victims.

One night, however, the husband awakened ill. Expecting his spouse to rouse from sleep and soothe him, all he found was her satiny skin spread like a sheer skirt across the chair of her dressing table. Understanding at once the significance of this terrible find, he knew what he must do despite his illness.

Fetching a container of salt from the pantry, he liberally salted the delicate skin inside and out, then placed it across the chair in front of his wife's dressing table, making sure to leave every fold just as she had arranged it. He then lay back down and waited for the hag's return.

Flitting breathlessly through her open bedroom window in the light of the silvery three-quarter moon, the hag reached for her skin and slipped it on, then gazed at her moonlit form in the mirror of her dressing table. The skin glowed milky white and fit more smoothly than a glove.

Suddenly, she let out a cry of terrible pain. From her lovely, silky skin came the acute burning sensation of salt poured in an open wound. She longed to throw the skin off but did not dare, for her husband and tormentor had leaped out of bed and lit the bedside lamp at the instant she cried out.

Writhing in agony, the hag stumbled into the bathroom and turned on the taps, filling the claw-foot tub with cool water. She felt the tiniest relief as she slid in. But ultimately, nothing could ease the burning sensation under her tender skin, neither the purest of lotions nor the endless milk baths in which she soaked. The hag remained confined to her room indefinitely, tenderly treating her beautiful, painful skin.

In another case, a hag was slipping into a locked smokehouse filled with delicious hams, fish, sausages, and other expensive meats. Every night, she ate her greedy fill. Before long, she nearly depleted the stock of the smokehouse.

The owner checked the lock of the smokehouse many times and even sat up several nights, shotgun in hand, keeping watch for the culprit, while his smoked delicacies continued to disappear. After finding his precautions had no effect, he determined that the culprit was none other than a crafty, hungry hag and immediately set about finding her skin.

Having heard rumors that an old woman who lived nearby was a hag, the owner crept into her cabin late one night carrying a tin each of salt and pepper in his jacket pockets. He quickly saw the old woman's empty bed and the skin hung behind the cabin door. Taking the skin down, he dosed it heavily inside and out with salt, then with pepper. Before slipping quietly outside, he hung the skin carefully back behind the door.

When the hag returned after eating her fill of delicious smoked meat, the first thing she did was reach behind the cabin door and slip on her skin. She had barely gotten it on when she cried out in anguish, "Skinny, skinny, why don't you like me?" Wincing and crying, she tried the skin on again and again, to no avail. It was simply unbearable to wear. She had no choice but to wrap herself in her bedsheets and lie shivering on her bed.

Rarely glimpsed, spoken of in hushed tones, and foolishly believed by many to have faded into obscurity, the hags and plat-eyes of Georgetown County still lurk after dark and prey on the unsuspecting. Whether bedding down for a good night's sleep or traveling a lonely plantation road after dark, low country residents and visitors are well advised to take care.

The
Hanging Tree

County was
once a wilderness punctuated by settlements, a place where frontier justice prevailed. One custom from those days that died
hard was lynching, a barbarous form of punishment practiced
even into the twentieth century. Unjust, spontaneous, and bru-
tal, lynching was always deadly—except for once, when something not quite human was hanged and did not die.

Many venerable trees predating the Revolutionary War grow
in Georgetown County. Some of the oldest are live oaks, which
do not shed their tiny leaves all at once but stay green year-
round. Early Englishmen, searching the low country for trees

with which to build the king's ships, chose hard-as-rock live oaks for the vessels' ribs. The oldest live oak in Georgetown's historic district is estimated to be six to eight hundred years old. The circumference of its trunk is twenty-three feet. This revered oak, growing in the rear garden of a home built around 1760, was already a large tree when the port of Georgetown was conceived in the early 1700s. Its long, graceful limbs were spreading over the back gardens of neighboring homes when Georgetown was occupied by the British in the Revolutionary War, then by the Federals during the Civil War.

Another evergreen that grows to massive heights in the low country is the magnolia, whose huge, heavy, cream-colored blossoms exude an intoxicating scent during the late spring and early summer. Though the exotic magnolia is strong and long-lived, it is primarily an ornamental tree—although it sounds incongruous to refer to a tree that can reach such towering heights as an ornament. By contrast, the beautiful, fast-growing, fragrant pine has long been considered a necessity for the production of lumber and of turpentine, tar, and pitch, otherwise known as naval stores. From early colonial days, the tallest, straightest pines were destined to become mainmasts on the king's ships.

The towering cypress has long been a staple of Georgetown architecture. While heart of pine was the requisite flooring for most plantation manors and townhouses before the Revolutionary War, cypress was the lumber of choice for exteriors. Cypress is nearly impervious to termites and highly resistant to the moisture that pervades Georgetown County. Much of the cypress lumber used for clapboard siding in early Georgetown homes is still intact over two centuries later.

One towering Georgetown County cypress proved useful during colonial days without ever being touched by a saw blade. Though the tree saw only intermittent use, its infamy grew over the course of the next two centuries. Even now, many decades since it was last put into action, this stately, beautiful cypress is known as "the Hanging Tree."

During the Revolutionary War, while the British occupied the port and the surrounding countryside, two Patriot soldiers were foraging for food in the western end of what is now Georgetown County. A zealous Tory, or British sympathizer, came upon them and shot them dead. Enraged Patriots in the immediate area lost no time in executing the Tory by hanging him from a great, long, horizontal limb of a nearby cypress tree.

A natural gallows, the limb of this cypress saw increasing use over the years. The country community where the cypress grew was sixteen miles outside Georgetown, far from the township's more ordered approach to justice. No one thought twice about where to take a criminal when an execution was in order.

It was Adam McDonald who took the old Indian path that ran beside the cypress and expanded it into a road. McDonald owned property seven miles deep and fourteen miles long in the vicinity of the Hanging Tree.

In a county of rice planters, the McDonalds were cattle barons. They cultivated some rice in their fertile fields along the

Santee River but devoted their major interest to livestock. Among the eighteen hundred head of livestock on their plantation prior to the Civil War were at least a thousand cattle.

In the lean years after the war, the plantation lands adjacent to the Hanging Tree passed to other owners. Times had changed, but an occasional wrongdoer still met his fate at the tree in accordance with the unofficial "lynch law," which bypassed arrest, judge, and jury. Although feelings were mixed about lynchings, they were generally accepted as a necessary evil and a deterrent to crime. The *Georgetown Semi-Weekly Times* heartily condoned, on its front page, lynching as punishment for what was delicately referred to as "the usual crime," meaning rape. Murderers were generally arrested and given a fair trial. This was not the case with rapists. A man accused of this terrible crime was usually hanged quickly, with no arrest or preamble.

In the late 1800s, a stranger came into the tightly knit community of Lamberttown, which had grown up near the Hanging Tree. After only a short time in the area, this stranger perpetrated a crime—presumably a rape—so heinous that the law was not even notified. The locals felt that the best way to assure the safety of the rest of their womenfolk was to catch the stranger and hang him by the neck. This was the only way to be certain he would not escape to visit grief upon another victim, they agreed.

As soon as the stranger was caught, he was hauled by several strong men to the Hanging Tree. His head was placed in a rough noose at one end of a long rope. The other end was tossed high in the air over the heavy, well-worn limb of the old cypress tree. A horse-drawn farm wagon, hastily rolled under the great limb to serve as a platform, was held steady and the stranger forced to climb upon it. The determined men holding the other end of the rope took up the slack as the stranger mounted the wagon, making sure he was held upright and had no chance to slip or twist away. As soon as his footing was steady, the wagon moved away. The bitter crowd watched, expecting to see the stranger receive the cruel reward for his equally cruel crime—expecting to hear the final crunch of his bones. That sound never came.

Out of the sky—which moments before had been a cloudless blue dome—arose a massive thunderstorm, its violent wind whipping rain around the hanged man. As thunder boomed and lightning cracked ominously close to the crowd, the stranger worked furiously to loosen the noose. No sooner had he pulled it wide enough to squeeze his head out than he fell to the wet ground, jumped up, and dashed away. The stranger—who by all accounts should have been dead—was never seen or heard from again.

For years, the horrified witnesses pondered this event in their hearts. A properly hanged man had gotten down and run away before their very eyes. They wondered if perhaps he really had been dead and escaped nonetheless—if he was something inhuman that could not be killed by hanging. After all, he had perpetrated an inhuman crime.

———

The tree's notoriety grew after this event, causing many a shiver as residents and travelers passed under—for there was no easy way to avoid it—the overhanging limb of the cypress.

When U.S. 17-A, or Saints Delight Road, was paved and widened, taking the place of the old road, it was constructed around the Hanging Tree, passing right under the limb where so many had been lynched.

Once, a traveler headed for Charleston on the new highway stopped to ask a Lamberttown resident about the legendary Hanging Tree. When the resident finished telling the history of the tree, the frightened man drove back to Andrews and went to Charleston via Georgetown, driving many miles out of his way to avoid passing under the lynching limb.

The great, old, moss-covered limb continued to cast its shadow over the lonely stretch of highway until an unusually high-bodied truck tore it away with a great, sudden cracking sound. This occurred several decades ago. Fortunate not to have wrecked his truck or been injured in the mishap, the driver was, it is said, arrested and put in jail for so defacing the Hanging Tree. Despite deep local resentment for the damage to the historic cypress, he was let off with a fine. Nothing, however, could replace the centuries-old limb where so much frontier justice had been meted out.

The Hanging Tree still looms beside the highway in Lamberttown. It is obvious from some distance away. Wrongdoers no longer need fear a lynching when in the vicinity of the Hanging Tree, but travelers continuing several miles down U.S. 17-A toward Jamestown should beware a notorious and unforgiving speed trap immediately after crossing the bridge over the Santee River.

Unmistakable as a gallows despite the loss of the hangman's limb, the cypress remains outstanding and conspicuous. Its imposing presence is an eerie reminder of the many long-ago lynched criminals whose energy still lurks, shadowlike, around the lush green reaches of the legendary Hanging Tree.

The Hanging Tree is approximately 16 miles west of Georgetown. From U.S. 17 just south of the Georgetown city limits, turn right onto Pennyroyal Road. After 10 miles, turn left onto Saints Delight Road (U.S. 17-A). The Hanging Tree is on the right side of the highway after 6 miles.

Kinloch

The old, tree-shaded plantation road that connects U.S. 17 with South Island Road has changed little over the past two centuries, save that now it is paved. As the narrow, two-lane route winds past Annandale, Millbrook, Wicklow Hall, Woodside, and Rice Hope Plantations, there is little to reveal that these grand places exist, except for narrow openings in the dense forests of pines and live oaks. These openings, some marked by only a weathered mailbox, begin as narrow dirt lanes and open onto wide, grass-lined, manicured avenues leading to plantation houses set miles back in the trees.

One narrow, sandy lane with spacious, grassy shoulders is lined by live oaks that are, in turn, flanked by large magnolias. This quintessential avenue cuts a straight, two-mile swath through the pine forests to the sixty-acre lake beside which the house at Kinloch Plantation resides.

Kinloch House is separated from the lane by a thick, tall stand of bamboo called a canebrake, which serves as a natural privacy barrier on many low country plantations. Behind the canebrake, the house rises steeply, a two-story white clapboard gem of a lodge crowned by a widow's walk and graced with four chimneys, one on each end of the main house and one each on the east and west wings.

Built in 1923 as a gun club and hunting lodge, Kinloch House replaced the manor house of Milldam Plantation, which burned in 1879. Milldam was purchased in 1912 by the Kinloch Gun Club. It and nearly a dozen other antebellum plantations of the North Santee River and the Santee Delta now form six-thousand-acre Kinloch Plantation.

Landscaped simply but elegantly with azaleas and camellias, the front garden of Kinloch House boasts an ancient magnolia so huge that one of its limbs—prior to breakage by Hurricane Hugo—was long, low, and wide enough for a man to walk upon it up into the lofty area of the tree. Leading to Kinloch's veranda steps is an expanse of beautifully maintained brick inlaid in the soil.

At various times during the year—and particularly during hunting season—Kinloch House is occupied by its Atlanta-based owners. But often, all eight bedrooms and the expansive living and dining areas are empty. It is during these times, when the house is locked up tightly, that those within earshot can hear a bedroom door in the east wing unexplainedly slamming shut. However, it is only when someone is inside the house that Janie makes her presence known in the old kitchen in the west wing.

For years, Janie was the undisputed cook of Kinloch. She had absolute sovereignty over the huge, cast-iron Garland stove that dominated the kitchen. No one questioned her authority, whether the owners of Kinloch were in residence or not. The owners sometimes requested certain dishes but often left the menu to Janie's discretion, trusting that her meals would be a delight to the palate. Janie's talents were also respected by guests and employees of the plantation.

She was noted for the precise placement of every utensil in her kitchen. From the largest skillet to the smallest measuring spoon, each item had a specific place, so that Janie could put any utensil to its proper use at a moment's notice. No one ever dared change the arrangement of Janie's kitchen.

During the winter, she came to work in her favorite royal-blue coat. She often kept it on while waiting for the big, gas-fired stove to warm the kitchen.

Janie held her cherished position until she died at a fine old age. In fact, she enjoyed her status so much that she never quite gave it up despite her death.

Her successor in the Kinloch kitchen was Irene. Just as Janie had, Irene arranged all the utensils to suit herself and expected no one to displace them.

One morning not long after she took over, Irene came into the kitchen and saw that several pots and saucepans had been rearranged. They were not merely out of place, they were exactly as they had been when Janie was in charge! Irene looked around in disbelief. Who could have done such a thing?

Just then, a flash of royal blue at the kitchen door caught her eye. It was the tail of Janie's coat rounding the corner!

Irene quickly followed. Just ahead, she caught a glimpse of the royal-blue fabric grazing the corner that turned into the dining room. Dashing to catch up, she reached the dining room just in time to see the blue tail of Janie's coat disappear past the doorframe leading from the main hall into one of the west-wing guest bedrooms.

Irene knew the bedroom had only one door. Approaching cautiously, she stepped into the room. There was no one to be seen. The bedroom, with its neatly made twin beds and old-fashioned wide-slatted venetian blinds, was as empty as it had been since the last guests left. Frustrated, she walked back to the kitchen and began arranging it once again to her specifications.

Her experience with Janie began to be repeated regularly. Although a bit put out at not seeing anything but the tail of Janie's coat and kitchen utensils rearranged the old way, Irene was never frightened. She came to expect Janie's occasional visits. After each of them, she determinedly put the utensils back the way she liked them.

Not one to keep such experiences to herself, Irene told her fellow workers at Kinloch about Janie's activities in the kitchen and her disappearances. No one was particularly surprised. Workers at Kinloch Plantation had by then come to accept that they trod haunted territory.

Plantation hands were used to the large, unseen dog that often sidled up to lean, in typical friendly canine fashion, against their legs in the vicinity of Kinloch's avenue of oaks. Many a new plantation worker had felt an initial rush of terror when the weight of the ghostly dog pressed against his or her thigh, only to be informed by fellow employees that it was the unseen dog.

And anyone who takes a break from field work to rest on the bluff under one of the several shade trees will be the object of physically thrown twigs and verbally hurled epithets from up in the branches. This is Little Boy Hill, where, for as long as anyone can remember, the ghost of a young man has sat in the tree branches and scolded anyone who chanced to laze or even rest from labor on the hill under his tree.

Most of the old plantations that comprise Kinloch's expansive acreage had a slave graveyard. Long unused, these cemeteries are now overgrown and nearly forgotten.

It is on a narrow dirt road near one of Kinloch's slave graveyards that much unrest occurs. The cemetery is virtually unmarked, as nearly all the grave markers were made of wood that deteriorated over the years. On the other side of the dirt road is a pre–Civil War white cemetery. Over the years, plantation employees have seen hair-raising sights on the old bridge and the dirt lane near these burial grounds.

Close to the two cemeteries, the dirt lane is broken by a creek. For decades, the old bridge crossing this creek has been haunted by a coffin hovering in the air. And the ethereal figure of a man dressed in black and white and wearing a tall black hat has been seen on the lane near the bridge. So vivid are these apparitions that more than one Kinloch employee has run his vehicle off the road at the sight of them.

The old dirt road is one of the interior lanes that traversed the antebellum plantations. Workers used these roads to go from one plantation to another.

In the intricately woven slave societies, there were many marriages and liaisons between slave men and women who did not belong to the same plantation. Short leaves of absence were often granted to men whose wives and families lived on nearby plantations. Such was the case for one slave couple blessed with several children. The husband spent every leave of absence, no matter how short, with his wife and children in their cabin on the plantation where they lived.

It was during one of these visits that the husband became gravely ill. Believing his death was near, he insisted that he be buried on the plantation where his wife and family lived, where he felt himself to be at home. Slaves set great store by funeral rites and particularly by where they were buried. The husband insisted that, in order to rest peacefully, he must be buried where his wife would one day be laid to rest, too.

The husband passed away soon after making his request. Preparations were made to bury him in the slave graveyard of the plantation where he had died. However, as soon as word of his death reached the plantation where he had lived and work, his master sent a wagon pulled by two mules to bring the body back for burial. Despite the fact that the husband had already been placed in a plain pine coffin and funeral plans were being made, his body was loaded on the wagon and taken down the narrow dirt lane he had trod so many times.

When the wagon reached the bridge spanning the creek, the mules refused to cross. The driver was taken aback. He had driven the same pair of mules over the bridge many times and had never seen either of them show the slightest qualm. Indeed, he carried no whip because he had never found occasion to use it on the docile beasts.

He finally smacked the mules smartly with the long leather reins, but they still would not budge. They merely pawed the air and whinnied piteously. Exasperated, the driver hopped down from his seat and strode to the front of the wagon. He took hold of the mules' bridles and pulled with all his might. They would not budge. Shaking their heads to free the driver's grip on their bridles, they backed away from him and the bridge, rolling their great, dark eyes in fear.

The driver then ran quickly to seek his master, leaving the mules, the wagon, and the coffin on the far side of the bridge.

The two men soon returned. Finding no more success getting the mules across the bridge than had the driver, the master sent for four strong field hands, who took the coffin off the wagon and bore it across the bridge.

The driver then climbed back onto the wagon and drove the now-docile mule team across the bridge.

No attempt was made to load the coffin back onto the wagon. A grave had already been dug in the slave cemetery in preparation for the body. Following their master's directions, the field hands carried the coffin into the cemetery, lowered it into the grave, and covered it with earth.

The dead man's friends and family held a graveside service for him the following day, singing him on to the Promised Land with beautiful spirituals. His wife, however, feared that her late husband would not be at peace, as his body was buried where he had asked it not be.

Soon after the burial, a curious phenomenon started occurring at the bridge. Slaves using the lane began to whisper that, before getting close to the bridge, they could see a coffin floating above it. When they got closer, it disappeared. Most who saw the hovering coffin elected to turn back and go another, longer way.

Eerier still was the lone figure of a man dressed in a high hat and formal black and white who began to appear on the lane near the bridge decades later.

To this day, the coffin can sometimes be seen hovering above the bridge on the interior plantation lane, as the long-dead slave's spirit balks at crossing the creek.

His master, who had the coffin borne over the water by human hands when his mules refused, is still fated to walk the dirt lane dressed in the finery of his own burial. Unable to release his servant from bondage even in death, the spirit haunts the area near the bridge, making sure the servant stays in the cemetery of the master's—rather than the heart's—choosing.

Kinloch Plantation is on North Santee River Road approximately 14 miles south of Georgetown. The plantation is not open to the public.

The
Harvest Moon

Rear Admiral John Dahlgren, commander of the South Atlantic Blockading Squadron, sat in his small stateroom aboard his flagship, the sidewheel steamer USS *Harvest Moon*, expecting breakfast early on the morning of March 1, 1865.

Admiral Dahlgren had a couple of reasons to feel secure as he steamed toward the Atlantic through the shipping channel in Winyah Bay, several miles south of Georgetown. His flagship carried four twenty-four-pound howitzer cannons and a crew able to man them at a moment's notice. Ever wary of Confederate mines, then called "torpedoes," Dahlgren had been assured by Commander J. Blakeley Creighton of the USS *Mingoe* that the channel had been swept clean of all explosives.

The lone smokestack visible in Winyah Bay even to this day attests that Blakeley was wrong. And the mournful sounds that sometimes float across the water on moonlit nights are evidence of a would-be sailor unknown to even his shipmates, a soul whose peace has been disturbed.

President Lincoln had long trusted Dahlgren as a naval adviser and felt he would excel at sea. The two friends were close in age. Lincoln was helping Dahlgren dispel the myth that "scientist sailors" did not go to sea, much less become fleet commanders.

Dahlgren was known primarily for his work with naval ordnance. It was his uncannily on-target Dahlgren missiles that armed the USS *Monitor* in its epic battle against the CSS *Virginia*, formerly the Federal frigate *Merrimac*. More an administrator than a sailor, Dahlgren was appointed to command the Washington Navy Yard when all those ahead of him for the post chose the Confederate side at the beginning of the Civil War. He held this position until he received his appointment as commander of the South Atlantic Blockading Squadron through Lincoln's personal reference.

In the spring of 1861, it had become evident that an important part of the Federal war strategy would be a naval blockade of the Southern coast. This entailed patrolling 3,500 miles of coastline wherein lay at least 180 harbors and navigable inlets. With only 42 vessels to perform this ongoing task, the navy realized it needed more gunboats—specifically, gunboats small enough and with a shallow-enough draft to maneuver the coastal waterways. It began seeking out merchant vessels that met the size criteria and could be refitted to perform blockade duty.

The *Harvest Moon* was built as a merchant vessel in 1863 in Portland, Maine. On November 16 of that year, she was purchased for the Federal navy by Commodore J. B. Montgomery for the sum of $99,300. Following a three-month stay at the Boston Naval Shipyard while being fitted out for her new assignment, she was commissioned in February 1864, with Lieutenant J. D. Warren in command.

With her great sidewheel and tall smokestack, the *Harvest Moon* was an impressive sight as she steamed out of Boston on her first naval cruise. The 546-ton vessel was 193 feet long and had a 29-foot beam and an 8-foot draft. Assigned to the First Atlantic Blockading Squadron, she was anchored off Charleston by February 24.

Upon the steamer's arrival, Admiral Dahlgren came on board and decided to make her his flagship. He transferred aboard the *Harvest Moon* the next day. On June 7, the newly appointed flagship commenced her blockading duties off Charleston. Over the next nine months, her regular duty and responsibilities as a picket and dispatch vessel took her to Tybee Island, Georgia, then back into South Carolina to the North Edisto River, then finally to Georgetown in February 1865.

Frustration had long been growing in Georgetown as citizens began to realize that the Confederacy could actually fall. Since August 1861, Federal gunboats had been patrolling Winyah Bay and making their way up the rivers surrounding the port. Only sixty miles from Charleston, a major Federal target, Georgetown was guarded heavily.

For over three years, Confederate vessels had managed to elude the blockade and smuggle supplies into Georgetown by blanketing their lights or using the cover of fog. In extreme instances, two-masted wooden vessels had entered less-guarded Murrells Inlet, thirty-five miles north, and, their hastily dismantled masts temporarily replaced by the tops of massive pine trees, brought goods down the Waccamaw River into Georgetown.

In November 1864, nearly all of Georgetown County's defenses were sent south in an effort to save Charleston. Both Charleston and Columbia fell on February 17, 1865.

It was February 26 when the *Harvest Moon* steamed into Georgetown Harbor. The Stars and Stripes was raised above the city for the first time in the war. After three and a half years of defying the blockade, having their port taken by the Union was a sad blow to the people of Georgetown.

Upon his arrival, Admiral Dahlgren announced the end of slavery, and martial law went into effect. While great numbers of freedmen set out on their own as soon as possible, many others, never having known a life in which they were not provided food, clothing, shelter, and livelihood by their owners, were ill-prepared to face free living.

Once-wealthy plantation owners faced a destitute future, as the surrender of Georgetown withdrew from them the thousands of hands needed to plant, flood, dam, drain, harvest, and maintain the precise environment of the rice fields.

Since Federal agencies to help people make the transition from dependency to self-support were yet to be established, the rice planters of Georgetown County were told that they must, for the next sixty days, support the former slaves in the manner they had before the war. This requirement did not prove too difficult for those responsible for only a few freedmen but was nearly impossible for owners with legions of former slaves. The presence of the *Harvest Moon* in Georgetown Harbor was a sore reminder of this sixty-day decree.

No one resented the flagship more than Confederate captain Thomas West Daggett. Born in New Bedford, Maine, in 1828, he had come south as a young man. After apprenticing as an engineer in Georgia, he had moved to Charleston, where his first two wives died. The mid-1800s found him in the Waccamaw Neck area of Georgetown County. He married a local lady, Mary Tillman, with whom he eventually had six children. Daggett managed a mill on Laurel Hill Plantation, where local rice was pounded to ready it for the Charleston market.

In 1856, he became a captain in the South Carolina militia. Already a peacetime military veteran, he commanded the Waccamaw Light Artillery during the early part of the war.

Appointed head of Confederate coastal defenses from Little River south to Georgetown as the war was coming to a close,

Daggett took the surrender of Georgetown as a personal defeat. He resolved to do something about it.

On February 28, Federal marines captured Battery White, an earthen fortification that guarded the sea access to Georgetown Harbor and the Santee River from its elevated position on Mayrant's Bluff. The *Harvest Moon* anchored overnight at Battery White to give Admiral Dahlgren the opportunity to investigate the newly taken fort.

That same night, Captain Daggett was wide awake. In the upper story of Stephen W. Rouquie's harbor-front business, located next to the Town Clock in Georgetown, he was busy constructing a torpedo from a percussion cap and a keg of black powder.

In the early-morning hours of March 1, the mine was finished. Captain Daggett floated his creation out of Georgetown and into Winyah Bay's shipping channel a few hours before the *Harvest Moon*, accompanied by the tug *Clover*, weighed anchor and left Battery White, heading toward the Atlantic.

As he waited for his breakfast that fateful morning, Admiral Dahlgren had every reason to feel secure. He had, however, underestimated the strong emotions flowing through the surrendered port town behind him.

Shortly before eight o'clock, the *Harvest Moon*'s steel hull was rocked by a tremendous explosion. She began to sink. Crew member John Hazzard, rank unknown, was in the hold and was killed instantly. He was the only known casualty.

It was not immediately clear what had happened. Only after

being ferried by the *Clover* to the USS *Nipsic* did Admiral Dahlgren piece together the rapid events of the morning in a formal report to Secretary of the Navy Gideon Welles.

REPORT OF REAR ADMIRAL DAHLGREN, U.S. NAVY, REGARDING THE LOSS OF THE USS *HARVEST MOON* BY THE EXPLOSION OF A TORPEDO

Flag-Steamer *Nipsic*,
Georgetown Roads, March 1, 1865

Sir: My latest dispatches had been closed, and not hearing anything from General Sherman at this place, I was on my way to Charleston, but was interrupted for the time by the loss of my flagship, which was sunk by the explosion of a torpedo.

This took place at 7:45 A.M. today and the best information I have now is from my own personal observation. What others may have noticed will be elicited by the court of enquiry which I shall order.

The *Harvest Moon* had been lying near Georgetown until yesterday afternoon, when I dropped down to Battery White two or three miles below, intending to look at the work and leave the next day.

Accordingly, this morning early the *Harvest Moon* weighed anchor and steamed down the bay. She had not proceeded far when the explosion took place.

It was nearly 8 o'clock, and I was waiting breakfast in the cabin, when instantly a loud noise and shock occur[r]ed, and the bulkhead separating the cabin from the wardroom was shattered and driven toward me. A variety of articles lying about me were dispersed in different directions.

My first impression was that the boiler had burst, as a report had been made by the engineer the evening before that it needed repair badly. The smell of gunpowder quickly followed and gave the idea that the magazine had exploded.

There was naturally some little confusion, for it was evident that the vessel was sinking, and she was not long in reaching the bottom.

As the whole incident was the work of a moment, very little more can be said than just related. But one life was lost, oweing [sic] to the singularly fortunate fact that the action of the torpedo occur[r]ed in the open space between the gangways between the ladder to the upper deck and the wardroom which is an open passageway, occupied by no one, where few linger save for a moment.

Had it occur[r]ed farther aft or forward the consequences would have been fatal to many.

A large breach is said to have been made in the deck just between the main hatch and the wardroom bulkhead.

It had been reported to me that the channel had been swept, but so much has been said in ridicule of torpedoes that very little precautions are deemed necessary and if resorted to are probably taken with less care than if due weight were attached to the exsistence [sic] of these mischievous things. . . .

I have the honor to be, respectfully, your obedient servant,

J. A. Dahlgren
Rear Admiral, Comg. South Atlantic Blockading Squadron

Like many Georgetonians, Captain Daggett returned to the

rice business before the economy forced him to seek another livelihood. As did a number of other Georgetown County war refugees, he then moved thirty-five miles north to Conway. There, in a case of true irony, he became the captain of a Federal snag boat that kept the Waccamaw River free of obstacles.

The only Union flagship sunk during the Civil War, the *Harvest Moon* still lies where she went down in 1865, her rusted smokestack protruding as much as seven feet above the waters of Winyah Bay at low tide. Her uppermost deck and all below it lie solidly encased in the bay floor.

Considering the roles played by Admiral Dahlgren and Captain Daggett in the demise of the *Harvest Moon*, it stands to reason that one of them might haunt her wreck. Neither does.

The story of her haunting is more ethereal, involving the delicate thread of a young life lost and quietly mourned, the fear of reprisal in the domain of the living, and the fear of unrest in the domain of the dead.

In 1963, representatives of the New England Naval and Maritime Museum in Rhode Island began a study of the sunken flagship's integrity. Divers from the museum calculated the size and shape of the wreck and the amount and density of the mud encasing it. Other divers—explosives experts from the Charleston Naval Base—explored the hull to make sure there were no live shells remaining. The study indicated that the *Harvest Moon* was intact and in remarkably good condition. Soon, the Southern Explorations Association was formed to raise the vessel.

Since the *Harvest Moon* lies close to the surface, raising her appeared to be a much less formidable task than that of salvaging the many vessels that had been raised from greater depths after being sunk for a longer duration. However, problems abounded in the form of inexplicable equipment failures. The navy formally abandoned the *Harvest Moon* on February 18, 1964, nearly ninety-nine years after her sinking. Shortly thereafter, the Southern Explorations Association relinquished its plan for raising her.

During the late 1960s, a commercial fisherman began setting crab traps around the *Harvest Moon*, hoping she might be a haven for crustaceans. Invariably, any trap he set near the old wreck became damaged, drifted off, disappeared, or caught no crabs. Though he decided to set the majority of his traps elsewhere, he continued to place a few around the wreck.

In hot weather, he always set and collected his traps between midnight and dawn, when his catch would stay coolest. The closer the moon's phase was to full, the better he could see and the quicker he could work.

One clear, warm, moonlit summer night, he was setting traps not far from the *Harvest Moon* when he heard a sound that chilled him through. A low, keening, unearthly moan that was not human, not animal, and not even very loud carried from the wreck through the balmy night.

This solitary fisherman, an intrepid outdoorsman, was familiar with the sounds of all local wildlife. He knew the voices of the shorebirds and woodland creatures, as well as the terrible sounds that trapped animals make. He knew the sound of the panther calling from the woods on nearby Fraser Point. The otherworldly moan he heard coming from the *Harvest Moon* was not any of these.

Unable to identify the eerie voice, he asked some fellow fishermen who lived at Hobcaw Barony if they had ever heard a similar sound while working in the bay at night. He knew that if anyone could tell him about the sound, these men could, for they were descendants of Friendfield Plantation slaves and had fished Winyah Bay all their lives.

The men immediately asked if he had been near the *Harvest Moon* when he heard the sound. When he nodded, the normally jovial fishermen became rather grim. "Never go near the *Harvest Moon* during the moon," they told him nearly in unison, shaking their heads gravely. "Never." None of them would give any further explanation.

Wondering how the fishermen knew he had heard the sound "during the moon," he asked them pointedly about it. They would not answer.

Unable to find the source of the mysterious sound, the solitary fisherman stopped setting crab traps around the wreck of the *Harvest Moon* and soon put it out of his mind.

Then one cold, frosty November dawn right before duck season began, he was passing the wreck while returning from the ocean with a nice catch of spot-tail bass. Eyeing the familiar rusty smokestack rising out of the bay, he realized it would make a perfect duck blind.

Sunrise on the first day of duck-hunting season found him crouched with his twelve-gauge shotgun on crossed two-by-fours he had wedged inside the smokestack. But as innovative as this duck blind was, it was too uncomfortable to use regularly. He left the two-by-fours in the smokestack and did not return until nearly two months later in the season.

What he found was very curious. Laid on the two-by-fours, safe inside the smokestack, were three pieces of broken crockery. Who had put them there? A chill colder than the icy January dawn ran through the solitary fisherman. Broken bits of family crockery, he knew, had long been used to adorn the graves in old slave cemeteries.

Rather than stepping on the crockery, he placed the three fragments in the pocket of his jacket. After a few hours of hunting, he left, taking the two-by-fours and the broken crockery with him.

Soon, shad season began, and he joined the groups of fishermen setting nets in the Waccamaw River just north of Georgetown. At the end of one successful day of fishing, he was enjoying a supper of mouth-watering shad stew with a group of black fishermen from Sandy Island. As the hungry men shared the feast, the moon rose over the river to replace a spectacular winter sunset. As the camaraderie grew around the stew pot and its warming embers, the solitary fisherman told the group about his puzzling and eerie experiences at the wreck of the *Harvest Moon*.

The Sandy Island fishermen, distant relatives of the fishermen from Hobcaw Barony, listened carefully to his words. When he finished recounting his tale, they told him the long-guarded reasons for the curious occurrences he had witnessed.

Just before the close of the Civil War, while the *Harvest Moon* was anchored in Georgetown Harbor, a young black man from Friendfield Plantation had made friends with the crew of the ship. When the capture of Georgetown had been finalized and he knew the flagship was leaving Georgetown for good, the young black man, scarcely more than a boy, had made a brave but ill-advised decision: he stowed away aboard the vessel that to him represented freedom.

Only his family members knew of the young man's secret adventure. Unable or perhaps unwilling to hold him back, they accepted his leaving with mixed emotions.

Upon hearing the shocking news that the *Harvest Moon* had hit a torpedo and sunk with one enlisted casualty, the youth's family hoped he had survived the disaster. But after a few days, when he did not return home, they knew he was dead.

The family dared not ask for his body to be recovered from the wreck, for that would mean admitting they knew of his plan to travel aboard a Federal vessel without permission. With the rapid change of local government from Confederate to Federal, with slavery barely over and Georgetown under martial law, their fear of a conspiracy charge was understandably great. The family mourned the lost young man in agonized silence.

The conjure woman of Friendfield was as disturbed about the young man's demise as was his family. Her distress, however, was of a different nature. She feared that the youth's spirit would not rest in the unhallowed grave of the great gunboat. A proper grave needed broken pieces of crockery placed reverently upon it to signify that the family had been broken, to keep evil spirits away, and, most of all, to keep the spirit of the deceased in the grave. Had the young man's body been brought back to his family members, they would have made sure he was buried decently and his grave marked with broken crockery so his spirit would sleep peacefully. After suffering his unfortunate fate, then being interred in the sunken wreck, the young man's spirit would surely moan, she knew.

Worse still, the conjure woman knew that during the brightest phase of the moon, which normally caused reflections to be seen in the water, anyone who looked into the bay above the old wreck would risk seeing clear into the world of the restless spirit on the other side.

She was determined that the young man's spirit not be left to moan with unrest. The only course was to give him some semblance of a proper burial immediately.

Soon, the conjure woman visited the wreck. From the wooden seat of her small rowboat, she saw there was no place to lay anything permanently on the young man's iron tomb. With a sigh, she ceremoniously dropped several carefully chosen pieces of broken crockery into the water directly above the *Harvest Moon*. Perhaps this would help the spirit to rest, she thought. But what would happen as the crockery was eventually shifted off the wreck?

Until she died many years later, the conjure woman made sure that a few pieces of crockery were placed at the site of the wreck every so often. After her death, her successors continued the tradition. That is why the solitary fisherman found broken pieces of crockery on the two-by-fours inside the *Harvest Moon*'s smokestack.

But what keeps the young man's spirit at rest when the crockery disappears and none has yet been brought to replace it?

During those intervals, nothing soothes his disquieted spirit. That is when his low, keening, unearthly moan carries through the moonlit night over the place where Winyah Bay is broken by a lone smokestack.

The Harvest Moon *lies 3 miles south of Georgetown on the bottom of Winyah Bay. The wreck is accessible only by boat.*

Cape Romain Lighthouse

Just off Cape Romain lies lonely Raccoon Keys, now known as Lighthouse Island. Near the center of the island stands the black-and-white Cape Romain Light, a glorious reminder of the days when ships depended on lighthouses to keep them from foundering on dangerous shoals.

Although no beacon has burned in the lofty lantern room for over half a century, the beautiful sentinel can still be seen for miles by day. Over the last century, the lighthouse has listed more than two feet to one side. The keeper's cottage has been gone for many years.

A romantic air of loneliness surrounds the island. The once-manicured grounds have given way to overgrown paths winding among the majestic Cape Romain Light, a smaller, earlier lighthouse, and an untended old grave.

It is sad indeed that this lone grave had to be dug, for in it was laid to rest one who would not rest. Buried in this long-neglected plot is a woman who died an untimely, pointless, and cruel death at the hands of someone she loved, here on this wild and lonely island. Unable to accept her fate, the victim has long haunted her island home, her ghostly footfalls familiar to light keepers years after her death.

———————

The story of how the lighthouses came to be built and a grave laid nearby began in the nineteenth century.

In 1827, the federal government built a sixty-five-foot red-brick lighthouse on Raccoon Keys approximately ten miles southwest of the entrance to the Santee River. Its purpose was twofold: to warn ships from running aground on the dangerous shoals near Cape Romain and to aid southbound vessels attempting to steer clear of the Gulf Stream.

One reason ships had been running aground on the shoals was that an abandoned windmill on the cape was being misidentified as the Morris Island Light, located at the entrance to Charleston Harbor, farther south. Confused captains, believing they were entering Charleston Harbor, were soon at the mercy of the Cape Romain shoals. Plans to build a light atop the windmill were halted when no ground high enough for a keeper's cabin could be found nearby. Therefore, Cape Romain's lighthouse was built on nearby Raccoon Keys.

The original light received criticism for its height. Its lantern room was eighty-seven feet above sea level, and its light did not shine far enough to save ships from the dangerous shoals. In 1851, the Lighthouse Board recommended to Congress that Cape Romain have a new, taller tower.

In 1857, the government constructed another brick tower nearby. Laid on a foundation of timber pilings, the new octagonal structure stood 161 feet. Its bottom third was painted white, while the eight sides of the upper two-thirds were painted black and white alternately. The new beacon shone far up and down the coast and into the Atlantic.

During 1861, in an effort to keep Federal troops from making use of the new lighthouse, Confederate soldiers destroyed its lantern and costly Fresnel lens. In 1866, this damage was repaired and the lantern relighted.

Three years later, cracks began to show themselves in the walls of the tower. By 1873, more cracks were apparent, and the district engineer discovered that the lighthouse had taken on a slight lean to the west that misaligned the lens by twenty-three inches. Careful adjustment brought the lens back to its correct level, but within a year, the lighthouse leaned nearly four more inches. No additional settling occurred until 1891, when adjustments were made once more.

The Cape Romain Light was deactivated in 1947. During the late 1950s, the keeper's quarters were removed, leaving the tall, black-and-white octagon and its smaller red predecessor the only structures on the island.

<hr />

No keeper mans the Cape Romain Light now, but in bygone days, a neat frame house ringed by a white picket fence rested at the base of the tower. This cozy dwelling was where each keeper of the light lived with his family while fulfilling his responsibilities in maintaining the beacon.

Many decades ago, a light keeper named Fischer lived in the cottage with his wife. The couple was Norwegian, and as beautiful as life was at Cape Romain, Fischer's wife missed the old country and wanted nothing so much as to travel back home on a visit.

Fischer's wife had been married before; she was a widow when they met. Her first husband had left her an inheritance of jewelry and gold. This treasure, she felt, was her ticket back to Norway. Fischer, however, was against it. He adamantly refused to let his wife make the journey.

This disagreement grew and grew. Though Fischer and his wife rarely referred to it, it was always there between them. The gold and jewelry that Fischer's wife wanted to use to finance a trip rested heavily on both their minds. Being isolated together at their beautiful home on the island was torture for them both.

Their discontent reached its peak one wild and stormy night as the wind howled and the ocean raged. Both Fischer and his wife gave voice to their anger, until their fury was as great as that of the storm blowing outside.

Finally, in a fit of anger, Fischer's wife gathered her precious gold and jewels and rushed out into the storm to hide them. A short time later, she came back to the cottage smug and defiant, unaware that her husband was waiting with their largest, sharpest butcher knife. Moments later, she was dead, her blood seeping into the wooden floor of the cottage.

This was long before the days of sophisticated forensics. No one was able to dispute Fischer's insistent—though highly questionable—claim that his wife had committed suicide. It was only years later that the old light keeper told the truth. In a deathbed confession, he described how he had waited for his wife to reenter the cottage that stormy night and plunged the butcher knife into her breast.

Through the years, the grave of Fischer's wife was tended by a succession of light keepers. These men grew used to the lingering presence pervading the Cape Romain Light. On calm nights, when there was no wind to howl down the lighthouse's 195 steps, a keeper going about his duties in the lantern room might chance to hear footsteps near the head of the stairs. But opening the trapdoor and shining a lantern down the spiral steps always revealed the same thing: nothing.

August Fredrich Wichmann, the keeper of the Cape Romain Light for twenty-one years during the early 1900s, had this experience many times. His son, who was born at the lighthouse, believes the mysterious footsteps belong to Fischer's wife, whose murder was never answered for and whose grave still lies in the place she wished to leave. He vividly recalls seeing the old bloodstains on the floor of the keeper's cottage, a sight he witnessed as a child.

Unable to rest peacefully near the scene of her violent, unjust, and unavenged death, the spirit of the light keeper's wife is a permanent presence in the darkened octagon of the Cape Romain Light.

The Cape Romain Lighthouse stands on Raccoon Keys, also known as Lighthouse Island, approximately 40 miles from Georgetown. It is accessible only by boat.

Spirits of
the Chicoras

Igmu Tanka Sutanaji is commonly known as Gene Martin, chief of the Chicora Indians of South Carolina. Chief Martin does not believe in ghosts. However, he does believe in spirits. In fact, the wisdom of the ancient Chicora spirits has been instrumental in guiding him in reestablishing the Chicoras as a tribe more than two centuries after their closely knit society was torn apart.

How the ancient Chicora tribe came to grief is a story of

trust and betrayal. But due to the intervention of the spirits and the perseverance of Chief Martin, the Chicoras are flourishing as a tribe again.

Long before Europeans arrived, Indians roamed the low country. Of the seventeen tribes of the eastern Siouan family that lived in coastal South Carolina, six made their home in what is now Georgetown County. These were the Sewees, the Santees, the Sampits (or Sampas), the Winyahs, the Pee Dees, and the Waccamaws. They called their coastal haven Chicora. Their names are still visible in the rivers and the bay they lived along: the North and South Santee, the Pee Dee, the Waccamaw, and the Sampit Rivers and Winyah Bay.

Living in tribes allied to a chief and his council, families relied on fishing, hunting, and farming for their sustenance.

The Chicoras gathered shellfish and caught many kinds of delicious freshwater and saltwater fish, spearing them, shooting them with bow and arrow, or catching them with traps, nets, or bare hands. Fish not cooked and eaten immediately were smoked and stored.

They hunted deer with finely crafted bows and arrows. The bows were made of oak and strung with two-finger-wide thongs of skin cut from the back of a stag. Fired from these powerful bows were arrows tipped with carved and filed bone, stone, or shell. Among the game the Indians sought were wild turkeys and other birds, the smaller fowl being shot with specially crafted miniature arrow tips. Although deer were prolific, the Chicoras often had to follow them all day, since they hunted on foot. Stags were hunted for their meat and hides, but does were cultivated by the Chicoras. Fawns were kept in the village while their mothers were allowed to forage in the forest all day, returning in the evening to suckle their young and be milked by the Indians, who made cheese from the milk. The Chicoras also kept ducks and geese in their villages.

Their gardens yielded potatoes, pumpkins, onions, beans, squash, and herbs. A staple of the Chicoras' diet, corn (maize) was grown in fields tended by both men and women. They used large conch shells attached to wooden handles for hoes. Guards were posted day and night to protect the precious maturing corn against consumption by wild animals. Every effort was taken to make the corn supply last until the next year's harvest. Stored free from dampness in great wooden cribs with ventilated floors resting on stilts, it was meted out to the tribe by the chief. Villagers ate their corn parched or pounded it into cornmeal for mush or cornbread. The Chicoras placed great emphasis on the planting and gathering of corn, holding a great festival at planting time as well as at harvesttime. The Indians also gathered wild honey, berries, plums, acorns, and other nuts to supplement their diets.

The Indians of Chicora lived in harmony with the low country for hundreds of years. But the moment European explorers set foot on the shores of their homeland, the Indians' way of life began to change. Known as fierce fighters in their struggles with other Indian tribes, the Chicoras were friendly and helpful to the Europeans, a well-intentioned attitude that hastened their devastation.

In 1521, Spanish explorer Francisco Gordillo was studying the lower Atlantic coast of North America, his expedition financed by Luis Vasquez de Ayllon, a Spaniard who had come to Hispaniola two decades earlier and grown wealthy in sugar cultivation and gold mining. Although the Spaniards by then controlled the Indies—as they referred to Hispaniola and other nearby Caribbean islands—they remained as interested in exploration as they had been decades earlier when Christopher Columbus made landfall in the New World.

Driven by a fierce storm to what is now Pawleys Island, Gordillo and his men anchored their two caravels and rowed ashore. The members of a small coastal tribe of Indians came to the ocean's edge to greet them. Upon contact with the newcomers, the natives rushed away into the forest, but not before the Spaniards captured a man and a woman and took them aboard one of their vessels. After being dressed in European clothing, lavished with gifts, and returned to their tribe, the two Indians assured the others that the strangers were friendly and generous.

The Indians then welcomed the Spaniards to Chicora, treating them as honored guests and giving them the finest fruits of their land: pearls, beautifully tanned animal skins, silver, and food. Some 140 Indians subsequently accepted an invitation to be entertained aboard the anchored caravels. Sadly, the Indians' intuitive wariness of the strangers had been well founded. According to prior plans, Gordillo and his men weighed anchor. As soon as the Indians were secured, the vessels sailed south for Hispaniola, where the Indians were to be made slaves in the mines and on the sugar plantations.

Ayllon was furious when Gordillo arrived. Although he owned many slaves on Hispaniola, Ayllon had forbidden Gordillo to bring back captives from his explorations. The governor general of the Indies, Diego Columbus, son of Christopher Columbus, was consulted. He and his council declared that the Indians were free people and must be returned to their home.

In the meantime, one of the Indians converted to Christianity and became proficient in the Spanish tongue. Ayllon gave him a European Christian name—Francisco—but chose the surname Chicora, since that was the way the Indians referred to their coastal homeland. This man, Francisco Chicora, journeyed to Spain with Ayllon and so impressed the Spanish king and court with descriptions of Chicora that the king agreed to finance an expedition to start a colony there.

This settlement—the first by Europeans in North America— was begun in 1526. Ayllon brought six ships containing seven dozen horses and an estimated six hundred people, including black slaves, Indians, Spanish women and children, and several Dominican friars. Some of the Indians kidnapped with Francisco Chicora served as interpreters. Long used to speaking the dialects of several tribes, they had quickly become fluent in Spanish.

The settlement was planned for a location somewhere between

Winyah Bay and the mouth of the Santee River. But sixteenth-century navigation being what it was, the party landed over a hundred miles north of its destination, near the mouth of the Cape Fear River. Here, the largest of the six ships was lost, an early casualty of the treacherous Cape Fear shoals. The remaining ships, which were smaller, easily sailed into the Cape Fear River, where the horses and many of the men went ashore. Finding themselves in the vicinity of their home for the first time in five years, Francisco Chicora and the other Indians wisely took the opportunity to leave their captors.

Realizing he had landed too far north, Ayllon headed south, the five ships sailing along the coast and the soldiers and horses following an Indian trail. Upon reaching their destination in late summer, Ayllon and his party settled just across Winyah Bay from Georgetown, at the mouth of the Waccamaw River. They named their colony San Miguel.

By the fall, many of the colonists succumbed to malaria, depleting the San Miguel colony. Among those who perished was Ayllon, who died on October 18.

Lulled by the semitropical summer and the mild fall, the surviving settlers were not prepared for the icy Atlantic winds that brutalized their settlement that winter. Thoroughly defeated, the colonists exhumed Ayllon's body and set sail for Hispaniola. Seven men froze to death during the voyage, and Ayllon's body was swept overboard in heavy seas. Only 150 of the original 600 settlers lived to make landfall on Hispaniola in early 1527.

Although left with a strong sense of distrust and at least one heretofore unknown disease, the Chicoras continued to flourish for a century and a half. It was in the late 1600s and early 1700s that their relationship with the British became their undoing.

In 1665, eight British noblemen known as the Lords Proprietors were granted the coastal region from Virginia to the St. Marys River in southern Georgia. Winyah Bay and the land that is now Georgetown County lay precisely in the center of this grant. Settlers soon began to arrive, and trading for furs and deerskins with the Indians kept them coming.

The Chicoras initially enjoyed the lucrative fur trade and interacted easily with the newcomers. But dissension soon arose. Determined to realize a profit from every aspect of their Crown grants, the Lords Proprietors gave the settlers permission to sell Indians captured in battle. A duty of twenty shillings was placed on every Indian slave exported to the West Indies. When an Indian was to be sold, no one could prove whether he had been taken in battle or simply kidnapped from his tribe. Many Chicoras were sold into slavery in Carolina, other colonies, and the Caribbean islands. The old slave market in Charles Town, later infamous for the tremendous number of African slaves sold there, was built for the Indian slave trade. South Carolina began exporting more Indian slaves than any other colony.

Fear for their families drove many Indians into slavery. One cruel ploy of slave traders was to approach an Indian village, seize a child from a group playing outside the lodge, and cut the child's arm off or set him or her on fire. When the adults in the village rushed to the child's rescue, the slave traders threatened that unless selected members of the tribe came with them peacefully, other village children would suffer the same fate.

Contact with English settlers brought new ailments like measles, typhus, and smallpox. In their effort to eradicate certain villages, the Lords Proprietors' men went so far as to take blankets from Indians prostrated by smallpox and give them as gifts to people in other villages. Soon, the Indians in these villages, too, lay dying.

There were a few notable exceptions to the poor treatment of the Chicoras by European settlers. A prime example was the colony of approximately 180 French Huguenot families that settled in the region of the North and South Santee Rivers. Protestant refugees fleeing the violently enforced Catholicism of their homeland, the Huguenots had immense respect for the Indians and no desire to compromise their freedom. After purchasing, rather than claiming, land from the Santee Indians, the Huguenots lived in harmony and friendship with them. The Santees were considered by some to be warlike, but the Huguenots would never have known it. Indeed, the area soon became known as French Santee.

Between enslavement, battles with settlers, relocation, and disease, over 80 percent of the 1,000,000 Southern Indians died. Entire tribes were eradicated. The Indian census of 1715 revealed that only 57 Sewee Indians were left and that the Winyah Indians had 106 tribe members in their lone remaining village. The census also found that the Santee Indians had only 43 warriors remaining; some of those 43 were killed in a battle with settlers two years later, and others were sold as slaves to the West Indies. The Sampit Indians all but disappeared. The Pee Dees are not mentioned in local records after 1753. It is believed that many of their number may have, for the sake of survival, joined the Catawba tribe of northwestern South Carolina.

Warring between tribes also exacted a toll on the coastal Indians. Many of the tribes were old enemies, and the intercession of settlers often increased this animosity. In 1711 and 1712, Colonel John Barnwell led South Carolina settlers and Winyah and Pee Dee Indians against the Tuscaroras of the Cape Fear River region. In this and other documented cases, the conquering Indians sold members of the defeated tribes into slavery.

The Waccamaws—the most numerous of the Georgetown-area tribes, with six villages and 610 people on Waccamaw Neck—declined sharply in 1720. A great number of their warriors were killed that year in a war in which the Winyahs sided with the settlers against the Waccamaws. Many surviving Waccamaw warriors were sold to the West Indies.

By 1720, the diverse coastal tribes were beginning to lose their separate identities. One of the last recorded activities of the coastal Indians occurred when Chief Eno Jemmy Warrior and a number of his men met with the Catawba tribe in 1743 as the government attempted to relocate coastal Indians northwest. By 1755, the tribes had all but disappeared.

Indians who acquiesced to the rules of the colonial government were considered free. Children of Indian slaves were considered slaves, too. Indians still living on their ancestral lands were forced to either leave the area or become "settlement Indians," meaning that they were expected to worship in the European Christian manner and work for the settlers, doing their gardening, hunting, and fishing. Many remaining Indians led quiet existences in the swampy areas of their homeland, living peacefully and humbly but not quite blending into the fringes of white society.

Vanished from their ancestral homeland were the Waccamaws, the Pee Dees, the Winyahs, the Sewees, the Santees, and the Sampits—or so it appeared.

The disappearance of the Chicora tribes would be too sad to relate were it not for one fact: the loving spirits of these native people never left. The proud spirits of the Chicoras still flourish, roaming and fishing along the rivers, hunting game in the primeval forests, and reveling in the comforts of their unspoiled villages.

These spirits are only a whisper of wind in the pines—except to those who can see them.

Gene Martin, chief of the Chicora tribe of South Carolina, spoke with me in reference to ghosts. He does not believe in them. He does, however, believe in spirits, for spirits are with him daily. One example is the cougar. Chief Martin's Indian name, Igmu Tanka Sutanaji, means "Great Cougar Stands Strong." "The cougar is with me constantly," Chief Martin said.

This cougar was never a living creature. "He has always been a spirit," according to Chief Martin.

Through their constant presence, their wisdom, and their guidance, the ancient Chicora spirits have been crucial in Chief Martin's work. Reestablishing the tribe and gaining governmental recognition are goals Chief Martin was heading toward even before he was sure of his destiny. Years ago, the spirits of the Chicoras began to bring about his work for the tribe.

"From childhood to the present day," said Chief Martin, "I have, in my sleep, spoken a language which no one has ever understood. I have been asked by my wife, 'What kind of language are you speaking?' This is when the chief would come and visit me and we would be speaking in the native language. The chief was a living person at one time.

"When I first started experiencing spirits about me, it was kind of frightening to me, but after several visions of a chief, I learned to listen closely to what they were saying to me. The spirits walk with me, they talk with me, they lead me, they guide me on a daily basis. Every place I go, the spirits go with me. Some people might call them guardian angels. They comfort me," Chief Martin said.

"Sometimes, I can be riding down a highway or waterway or byway and I can see an entire village prior to European contact, with children running and playing, still living in the dwellings as we did five hundred years ago." These villages are tranquil and their inhabitants happy, according to Chief Martin. He says the spirits are not ghosts, but rather the vital essences of the Chicoras who once peopled the land.

"I believe that when the spirit leaves the body, we simply walk into a third dimension here on earth," Chief Martin said. "The spirits of all our people live here in a third dimension. You walk through an invisible wall, then you are with your ancestors, I believe."

Since 1987, Chief Martin has worked tirelessly to reestablish his tribe in its ancestral homeland. Elected chief of the tribe by the Council of Native Americans of South Carolina, he was later elected by his own people—and chosen by the spirits—as the lifetime spiritual leader of the Chicoras. All members of the growing Chicora tribe can trace their lineage back to 1850, the prerequisite to being a tribal member.

Many years ago, Chief Martin's ancestors declined to leave the low country. Instead, they lived in tandem with white society while steadfastly retaining their Indian ways within the privacy of their families. Although Indians are members of a distinct race, census records for many years offered Chicora descendants no recourse other than to be labeled white or black. Chicora families allowed themselves to be listed as white but were careful to teach their children that their heritage was Indian and that their ancestors were the true natives of the land, having lived here before whites or blacks arrived.

Chief Martin has used this knowledge of his heritage as his inspiration. The Chicoras were not even acknowledged by the government when he came on the scene in 1987. Since then, he has taken them to being the only tribe in North America to have a day named in its honor by its state legislature.

Epitomizing the dignity and forthrightness of his ancestors, Chief Martin lives by the following creed: "Whenever I leave my home, I go in search of a friend. That way, I'll find no enemy."

May the spirits of the Chicoras that guide the chief be with him always.

The office of the Chicora Indian tribe of South Carolina is located at 25 East Main Street in Andrews, 18 miles west of Georgetown.